D1562389

Captivating Carla

Silver Foxes Romance

Kimberly Smith

Captivating Carla © 2022 All rights reserved. This book may not be reproduced or transmitted in any capacity without written permission by the publisher, except by a reviewer who may quote brief passages for review purposes.

This is a work of fiction. Names characters, businesses, places, events, and incidents are either the products of the author's imagination or used in a fictitious manner. Any resemblance to actual persons, living or dead, or actual persons living or dead, or actual events is purely coincidental.

This adult contemporary romance is recommended for readers 18+ due to mature content.

March 2022 Edition
ISBN: 9798441240024

Chapter One

Terrance's mother stood beside him as they watched Billy and Betty dancing. "He looks happy," she said, slipping her arm in the crook of his elbow.

Terrance had to agree. "Yes, he does." *I shouldn't feel jealous. This is my brother. I want him to be happy, but I want what he has.* It was clear that the woman in his arms loved him. It was in her smile and the way she looked at his brother.

"Maybe this one will work out for him. I also believe that we might have more little Watsons running around soon. If Carl ever settles down, maybe I'll get a couple more grandchildren." Terrance knew that his mother was referring to his younger brother and his new relationship. She continued, "Mike and Tanya's love is filled with such passion. They devour each other with their eyes. Your father and I were like that. That's how I ended up with four boys. If I hadn't had complications with Mike, there might be more of you, and I always wanted a daughter of my own. Now I'm going to have two," she said with a soft laugh.

Terrance had a vasectomy years ago, so there was no chance of him adding any new names to the family lineage. He didn't want children. Terry never wanted them. He didn't want to deal with diapers and playdates. He liked the life he was living. That was part of the problem with most women who pursued him. They were young enough to want families.

Lindsey had been one of those women, but she had also been after much more than a family. He sighed, thinking of her. Even though their divorce had not been amicable, he hoped she was happy.

His gaze shifted from the dance floor to other areas of the room. It stopped on the beautiful woman standing alone, looking around. He had seen her talking to Betty earlier, and Terrance assumed she was a relative or friend. He also saw her speaking with Nikki. *Who are you, pretty lady?*

"Dance with me?" His mother requested, interrupting his thoughts.

"Of course," he answered, leading her to the dance floor.

**

"Aren't there any grown single men here?" Carla asked as she joined Tanya, who stood by herself.

Her cousin pointed to a man dancing with an elderly woman. "You see the guy on the dancefloor?" Carla nodded. "That's the other brother, Terrance. I believe he's single."

"He's handsome," Carla said, tilting her head as she looked him over. "Are you sure that the biker brother is taken? He's more along the lines of what I need, someone who can get nasty in bed." *Plus,*

Terrance is the total opposite of what I've had most of my life.

Tanya shook her head, smiling. "He's got his eye on your sister, so *you* can forget about him."

"Is that so?" *For my needs, it really doesn't matter which brother it is.* "Since you and Betty are so in love after short courtships, I figure that the Watson men are well endowed and good in the sack. At least two are. Does it run in the family, I wonder?"

Tanya turned to face her cousin with her mouth hanging open. "OMG and everyone thinks I'm the freak in the family."

Carla smiled, "I'm not a freak, honey. I just haven't had any in a long time, and I'm determined to get laid before I leave Dallas. That's all."

"When was the last time you got some?"

"Two days after I was released from prison."

"That was – "

"Too damned long ago," Carla interrupted her. Carla's ex quickly put an end to her being on the market in Houston. Monster found out that she had been with someone and beat the guy into the ground. Once the word got around that Carla was off-limits, it was a wrap. Back then, she had still been terrified of him. *I didn't tell Tanya the whole truth. Each time I've gone out on the road, I've gotten some, but I'm tired of Tinder hookups. The young men I've come in contact with want me to do all the work. Since twerking became a thing, they expect women to put on a fucking show or act like I'm the star at a strip club. I don't have time for that mess. I need a man willing to work as hard as I do in bed. I love my cousin, but there are just some things I'm not ready to share.*

"I can offer you a discount code on a great little toy."

"No thanks. I intend to get the real thing tonight." Carla took in the handsome white man in the high-priced suit and smiled. *Yeah, he'll do for one night.*

She watched Terrance as he danced. Tanya must have peeped her looking at him again. "Well, I should warn you," Tanya said softly. "The Watson men have magic sticks. Once you climb on board, it is hard as hell to get off of it. That dick is like a Harry Potter wand. All he has to do is cast a spell, and you'll be seeing glowing deer and shit." Tanya giggled, waving her finger like a magician "Expecto orgasmium."

Carla giggled too. "You're special." Terrance was handsome in that distinguished, "I've got money way", not that his bank account mattered at all. She had more than enough money to take care of her needs. What she wanted was physical and animalistic in nature, but she was still slightly impressed. His clothing was high dollar, probably tailor-made just for him. Terrance moved easily as he danced with the woman that Carla assumed was his mother. She was far too old to be his date. Plus, she looked at him in that doting motherly way.

Carla smiled to herself. *He's a momma's boy.* Her smile faded quickly as she remembered that Monster was a momma's boy too. His mother was a viper, though.

This woman didn't look like she was deceptively kind, only to lure you in and sink her fangs into you, injecting poison into you until it disabled then killed you. Carla had mistakenly thought that she had found an ally when she met Millie, but it was only a matter of time before she realized that the apple didn't fall far from the tree.

Terrance's head raised, and he locked in on her. Carla didn't turn her eyes away. She wanted him to know she was watching him. Carla licked her lips slowly. *That's right, you can have me if you want, for one night only.*

Chapter Two

After dancing with his mother, Terrance led her to a table to sit and rest. "Would you like a drink?"

His mother smiled. "I would love one. How about a martini?" Terrance gave her a disapproving look. "Humor me. I know I shouldn't, but I'm not driving, and I'm not dead yet. I want one drink, that's all."

"Okay," he said, kissing the top of her head. He went to the bar and had the bartender prepare her drink, asking that he go easy on the alcohol. Even though his mother was in good health, she was on some medications that might not mix well with liquor.

While he waited, he glanced around. He spotted Mike coming back into the room. Then his eyes settled on the woman with the green scarf. Terrance was determined to meet her before the night was over. He took his mother's drink to her. "Will you be alright for a bit?"

His mother sipped and nodded her head. "You had them water down my drink, didn't you?"

"Who? Me?" Terrance asked, smiling.

Terrance still had not met Tanya yet. He wanted to, but from the moment they arrived at the party, he and his mother went to the gift table to add their gifts to the others. Then they spotted Billy and Betty dancing. He looked around for his brother, but Terrance didn't see Mike and Carl.

As he approached his brother, he said, "Where is Tanya? I think it's time that she and I meet."

Mike glanced around and pointed. "There she is."

She was standing with the woman he'd been eyeing while dancing with his mother. "Introduce me to my future sister-in-law."

"Not future." Mike cleared his throat. "We got married in Vegas last week."

"Are you kidding me?" Terrance said, grinning.

"No, I'm not, but we haven't told anyone yet. We want tonight to be about Darryl and Nikki."

"No problem. My lips are sealed," Terrance said, slapping Mike on the back. "Congratulations."

"Thank you," Mike said, leading them towards the women.

Terrance could tell immediately tell that he would like Tanya. Her easy and friendly smile warmed him. As he and Mike walked towards them, the face of the full-figured woman with purple hair lit up as she looked at his brother. *Mom's right. There are going to be little Watsons joining the family soon.* Terrance's gaze shifted to the woman beside Tanya.

She was elegantly dressed, meticulously groomed, and lovelier than any woman he had been interested in for a long time. She smiled at him. *Wow, she is stunning and single, I hope.*

"Terrance, this is Tanya," Mike said when they reached the women.

Terrance was prepared to shake Tanya's hand, but she opened her arms and hugged him. "It's a pleasure to meet you," she said. When she let him go, she introduced the woman with her. "This is my cousin, Carla."

Terrance took her hand, holding it between both of his. "Carla, it is a pleasure to meet you. It seems that we are destined to know one another, whether it is through Darryl and Nikki or via one of my brothers."

"It would appear so," Carla said, looking him in the eye. *Beautiful eyes and good eye contact.*

Before he could say anything further, Billy joined them. "Betty, this is my brother, Terrance."

Terrance removed his hand from Carla's reluctantly to take Betty's hand. "I must say that my brothers seem to have found the most beautiful women in Texas to fall for with the exception of one," he said, smiling at Carla.

**

This guy must have a Master's in B.S. It's one thing to be charming, but he is on the edge of being cheesy. It sounded like a line from a romance novel. Maybe he's not right for my mission. She looked around the room, checking out the other men. A few fell into the category of doable, but they all seemed far too young or attached for Carla's needs. She eyed Terrance again. He would have to be the one, but she needed to vet him first. "Terrance, why don't we get a drink and get better acquainted?"

He smiled at her. "That sounds like a great idea. Would you all excuse us?"

Carla couldn't help but look at Tanya as they walked away arm in arm. Tanya mouthed the words Expecto orgasmium. They crossed the room to the bar. The bartender quickly approached them. "What would you like?" Terrance asked Carla.

"I'll have a snakebite."

"Make it two," Terrance said with a smile.

I bet he's never had one before. "Careful now," Carla said, adding with a wink, "It's not a drink for the faint of heart. It'll make your balls drop." He was surprised by her comment. Terrance's eyebrows rose. Carla giggled. "What's that look for?" she asked.

"I – wasn't expecting you to say something like that."

"I hope you're not offended. I tend to say what's on my mind. I find it keeps from having miscommunications." Their drinks were put before them. Carla took hers, raising it. When Terrance matched her movement, she said, "To passionate possibilities." He smiled as they touched their glasses together and then drank.

He looked surprised as Carla downed hers and watched to see if he would do the same. Terry wasn't going to be outdone. He turned up his glass, drinking until the glass was empty. Carla almost burst out laughing at the face he made.

"Holy crap on a cracker!" The drink was extremely bitter and burned as it went down. He understood exactly what she meant by his balls dropping. "Wow, that is some drink." Carla was smiling at him. "Carla, tell me about yourself. What do you do?"

"Nothing very interesting. I work in the office of a small company in Houston. I manage the day-to-day operations. What do you do?" Carla had met men like him. They liked to talk about themselves and all that they had accomplished, what they owned and where they had been. It was written all over him, from his carefully quaffed hair, precisely trimmed mustache, and beard to his expensive suit, the Alessandro Galet Scritto Oxfords. Not to mention the Rolex on his wrist. Even his cufflinks screamed look how rich I am. *I bet he wouldn't miss one of the cufflinks if it went missing.*

Chapter Three

Carla opened her eyes just as the sun began to peek through the hotel window of the bedroom. Terry was snoring loudly behind her. She eased out of bed, tiptoeing around it to get to her clothes on the chair in the bedroom corner.

Once she was dressed, she grabbed the last two condoms on the nightstand before picking up her shoes and found a cufflink sitting in its toe. Carla glanced at Terry, a slow smile coming over her face. *I'll keep it as a souvenir.* She left the bedroom, slipping on her shoes, grabbing her purse and pashmina. Before Carla left, she tied her scarf around her head, hiding the bird's nest her hair had become after her sexual activities.

She let out a long breath of air as she waited for the elevator. *That man, that man.* Carla didn't know what to say, but Terry was phenomenal in the sack. *Let it go. It was a one-time thing. Push it out of your mind.*

She had no choice. He lived in Dallas, and she lived in Houston. They could never be any more than what they had the night before. Monster and his meddling would never allow her to have anything with anyone if it wasn't him, and it would never be him again. *Never!*

**

When Carla entered Betty's house, she hoped everyone was still in bed. Of course, Betty might have been at Billy's. That would mean that Aunt Gayle was the only one there. Carla was thankful that she had a key as she eased the door closed and quickly went upstairs to shower and change into a fresh set of clothes.

After her shower, styling her hair, and dressing in jeans and a tee-shirt, Carla went to the kitchen searching for a cup of coffee. She could smell the bacon as she crossed the dining room. Betty was at the stove, and Aunt Gayle was sitting at the counter. "Morning," they both said as she entered.

"Morning."

"What happened to you last night?"

Betty smiled and winked at her as Carla passed her to get to the coffee machine. The question had come from Aunt Gayle. *I can't tell the truth, but I won't lie.* "I met a stranger, and we had sex all night."

Aunt Gayle gasped and then tossed a dishtowel at Carla, "You are just awful. I almost believed you."

Carla grabbed a coffee pod and put it in the machine, added water to the Keurig, and pressed the brew button after placing a mug under the drip.

"Do you want some eggs?" Betty asked as she put the bacon on a platter.

"Sure, over easy."

"What time are we heading back to Houston," Gayle asked.

"I'd like to be on the road around one or two. I have a bunch of stuff to do at home."

"How's the job?" Betty asked as she cracked a couple of eggs. "You've been in the office for a while now."

"It's great. Though I love working in the office, I miss being on the road," Carla answered, getting a spoon from the drawer near her and taking her mug to the fridge to add cream.

"It's great that they still allow you to get on the road occasionally."

Carla took her cup to the table and sat down. Crossing her legs, she stirred her drink, watching as the black and white swirled together, changing into a caramel color. *I have too many secrets from the people who love me, but this is how it has to be.*

Chapter Four

Terry was frustrated with the report he was reading. For more than three weeks, the parts he needed to complete his company's latest product had been delayed.

His phone buzzed a minute later. "Mr. Noel on line one," Regina told him.

"Thanks," he replied before connecting to his business partner and friend. "Hey man, where are you?" His partner never went through his secretary unless he was out of the office.

"I'm on my way in. I was just calling to let you know that I'll be there in ten."

"Okay. Roman, I'm looking at a report that says the microchips that we need desperately are still sitting on a dock somewhere. We need them at the factory. What's going on?"

"The shipping company we've been using doesn't want to move such a limited amount of freight. I can't move the product from the port warehouse down south to the factory in Dallas. I'm looking for alternative shippers, but they have the same issue. If we had our own shipping division, we wouldn't have these problems."

"We can look at the bigger issue later. Right now, I need the pieces here to assemble the test models. There has to be a way to get this done. Look at some smaller freight runners if you have to."

"I have. I found one company. They are based in Houston, and I have heard nothing but good things from the people who recommended them, but something concerns me about this company."

"What's that?"

"Even though these people recommend them, they wanted me to know that all of the drivers are ex-felons."

Terry took a deep breath. "I can certainly see why you have reservations."

"It's not something the company is trying to hide. They seem to pride themselves on it, rehabilitation and whatnot. Maybe you should check them out for yourself. If you are okay with using them, I'm sure we can get the products to the factory quickly."

Ex-convicts? I need those parts, but do I want to take a chance on this company? His brother Carl was one, so he didn't have a problem with that per se. Of course, he had to factor in what others would think of his using that kind of company. His reputation was important to him. "Give me their information. I'll look into it and get back to you by the end of the day?" Roman gave Terry the name of the company. "Thanks," Terry said, ending the call.

He looked at the information on his notepad. His eyes stuck on the city. *Houston. That's where Carla is*. Terry hadn't been able to stop thinking about her since he woke up alone in the hotel bed the day after their tryst.

He was more than disappointed when he found that she had slipped away without him knowing. Carla had been very upfront about what she wanted, and it didn't include any further contact, but Terry hoped that after the night of passion and lust that they shared, Carla might be interested in something more. At the very least, maybe they could have another night together.

That had been days ago, and he considered calling her when Terry realized that he still had her number in his phone from when he texted her the hotel room number. The more he thought about it, the more sense it made to leave things alone.

They lived in different cities, and she obviously had only wanted to spend one night with him, or she would have left him a note or called him. He never did find his missing cufflink. Terry was certain that he put them both on the bedside table, but when he got dressed, one was missing. It seemed to have disappeared like the lone sock that always vanished between the washing machine and dryer.

He rubbed his chin, thinking about Carla and the missing jewelry. They were both a conundrum. Terry would have to give them thought later. He needed to find out what he could about the shipping company Roman suggested they use.

Terry googled 3P Shipping and clicked the link to the company's website. He read through the homepage, impressed with it. They were different than many companies because they specialized in freight shipping of less than truckload business, but they could accommodate larger shipments.

He clicked from page to page, more impressed as he went along. All Terry needed was to get his microchips from one place to another. Their website allowed you to enter the information and receive a quote without ever having talked to a live person. *Things have changed so much with technology.* He snickered at his thought. He was in the technology business, and it was because of the kinds of products he made that things worked differently.

So far, he had not seen anything alarming. He got to the bottom of the page. It wouldn't hurt to see what some of the employees looked like. The photos looked a little like passport pictures.

They all had the same boring grey background, and the executives had the same 'this is my work badge' smile. He scrolled further down and froze. Carla's picture was there under the title of Commercial Freight Operations Manager. *Well, well, well. What have we here? Operations manager? She made it sound like she was an office manager.*

The woman who still danced around in his thoughts was in the shipping business and worked for 3P Shipping. He didn't believe in coincidences. Maybe this was a sign that he could see her again. *That's wishful thinking, buddy. She was adamant about not pursuing anything further, but why?*

Terry wasn't sure, but he intended to find out. *Roman should be in his office by now.* He got up from his desk and went to Roman's office at the other end of their floor. He knocked on the closed door and strolled past Tara, Roman's secretary. She was on the phone but waved hello to him. "You got a minute?" Terry asked as he entered Roman's office.

"Sure. What's up?"

"How did you hear about 3P?" Terry stood instead of sitting, sliding his hands into his pockets.

"Two of the companies I called gave me their name. Why?"

Terry nodded his head. "Call 3P and set up an in-person meeting with the Manager of commercial shipping."

Roman made a face. "They have everything set up on the website. We can get a quote and do everything without going to Houston or having them come here."

"I know, but I want to meet with the manager. When you set it up, don't mention my name. Set it up as if you are the person they will be meeting with."

"Okay. What is this about?"

Roman knew Terry well. They had been friends for a long time. *I don't want to lie to him, but I don't want to tell him the truth either.* "I just want to check them out in person. Once I meet with her – err, them, we may do a contract for a longer-term."

Roman leaned back in the chair, folding his arms. "Her, huh?" neither said anything for a few seconds. "She must be hot if you're willing to see her in person." Roman sat up, moving the mouse around and typing.

Terry shook his head. *I should have known that he would pick up on the crap I was trying to feed him.*

"Oh, I see. Carla Baxter, the woman you would be meeting with, is very attractive but older than the women you normally date. I wonder if she's an ex-con?"

What? No. She can't be. She's too classy, sophisticated, and elegant. Not to mention she is in a management position. It was probably just the drivers that had criminal records. "No way."

"You never know. I can see why you want to talk to her in person. What if she's not single."

"She is, I think." *Crap, I was so busy thinking with my little head that I never asked if she was involved with anyone.*

"Wait, you said that as if you already know. Do you know this woman?"

Me and my big mouth. I've never been able to hide anything from him. Terry sat in the chair across from Roman. "My brother Mike just married her cousin. We met this weekend at an engagement party for Mike's son Darryl."

"Mmm, hmm."

"What?"

"You want some of that, don't you?"

Some more? Yes, I do. "No. She's practically family. I just want to see if we can work together."

"Then why are you making it a secret meeting?"

"It is not a secret thing. I just – *I'm no good at lying or keeping secrets.* Okay, okay. I'll tell you, but this is just between us." Roman crossed his heart and waited. "We had a one-night affair."

"You know what they say, 'Once you go black, you never go back.'" Roman grinned at him.

"Really? I expected more from you than old clichés."

"Sorry, dude. I couldn't help myself," Roman said, trying to stop smiling. "Have you ever dated a black woman before?"

"I've gone out with a few, but nothing ever came of it."

"If I knew you liked black women, I would have introduced you to my wife's friend or my sister for that matter. Hey, if things don't work out with Ms. Baxter, let me know, and I'll hook you up."

"Oh no," Terry said, getting up from his chair. "No offense, but I have enough help with being set up. It never works out. Just set the meeting up for me and do it quietly," Terry said, leaving Roman's office. *Everything is going to work just fine between Carla and me.*

Chapter Five

Carla opened the door to her office, leading Mr. Dierdre back to the front of the building. She shook his hand. "Thank you for coming in, Marcus. I'll be deciding about the position in a few days. We'll be in touch."

"Thanks," the man said, walking out the door.

Carla went to the reception desk to get the name of the next applicant. "Charles Sanders," the receptionist whispered.

"Mr. Sanders?"

"Yes, Ma'am." A black man said as he stood.

Carla gave him the once over. He was tall, in decent shape, and was dressed in slacks and a button-down. His clothing was cheap, but that didn't matter. He was neat and appropriately dressed for an interview, unlike the previous man who came in wearing a dirty tee shirt and Bermuda shorts. She held out her hand to him, and when he took it, he gave it a firm grip and shook. "I'm Carla Baxter; come with me."

She led him back to her office, closing the door after entering. "Have a seat," Carla told him as she moved around to sit behind the desk. As soon as the man's behind hit the seat, she pulled his resume from the pile on her desk and glanced over it. Carla looked at the notes she had written on it, noting that the address of his last employer was the address to the state prison in Teague, Texas. "How long have you been out?"

"Two weeks," he said after clearing his throat. She looked him in his eyes. *Show me who you really are. Can I trust you? Should I give you a chance or tell you that I'll get back to you.* To her surprise, the man on the other side of her desk didn't flinch or look away.

"Why should I hire you, Charles?"

"Please call me Chuck," he said, sitting forward in his seat. "Ms. Baxter, I spent ten years in prison, and I deserved to be there for what I did, but I've served my time. I don't want to go back to jail. I don't want you to hire me. I "need" you to hire me. I need to know that someone out here is going to see beyond who I was, and what I did, someone to give me a chance to show them who I've become. I am a hard worker. I'll do whatever you need done, as long as it's legal. I'll be the janitor, run errands, and answer phones. I don't care what job it is. I just want to work and be productive. You can contact any of the officers I served under at the prison. They will tell you what kind of worker I am."

Carla leaned back in her chair. She believed him. *I already know what you were convicted of.* She also knew that she would speak with his parole officer when necessary. "Chuck," Carla said, sitting up with her elbows on the desk. How did you learn about this company?"

"Terry Butler told me that I might be able to get a job here."

Carla knew Terry well. She hired him four years ago, and he had proven to be a great asset. She used her computer to pull up Terry's record. Then she picked up her phone and dialed his number. "Hey, boss lady," he said when Terry answered.

"Hey, Terry. I have a man named Chuck in my office. He says that you referred him for a job. Is that true?"

"Yes. He's a good guy. I'll vouch for him."

"Okay. How are things going on your run?"

"Great."

"How are your wife and the baby doing?"

"They are wonderful. I just wish I could get back on a local route so that I could be home more."

"Come see me when you get back. We'll see what we can do."

"Thanks."

"Take care," she said, ending the call.

"Chuck, since you have forklift training, I will give you an opportunity. If you fuck up once, you're out. I expect you to come to work, be on time, and prepare for your job the same as anyone else. I don't do special treatment unless it's earned. I need someone reliable and trustworthy. If you prove yourself, you can move up to a long-haul driving position when you are off parole. Right now, I'm going to put you on warehouse duties. Whatever the manager tells you to do, you do it. Starting pay is fifteen an hour, a minimum of forty hours a week. Be here Monday morning at eight."

Carla got up, offering him her hand. "Thank you, Ms. Baxter," he said, standing to shake it.

"I'll walk you out." Carla led him back to the front. Luckily Chuck was the last of her interviews for the day. "Tell Bowleg that Chuck Sanders will be reporting to him on Monday at eight. Then send a note to Erica that Terry gets a two-hundred-dollar bonus if Chuck completes his first month of employment without getting fired."

"Can I ask you something?"

"Shoot," Carla said, grabbing a piece of candy from the dish on the corner of the reception desk.

"How do you know who to hire and who to show the door. I've been here for three years, and I can't figure out how you know who will work out and who won't. We're all ex-cons. How do you know which ones are the right ones?"

Carla put the candy in her mouth, sliding it into the pocket of her jaw. She took a deep breath. "I don't know for certain. I have been wrong a few times, but the first thing is eye contact. If you can't look me in the eye, I can't trust you." *Monster never looked me in the eye unless he was about to fuck me or hit me. It was the only time that I saw the truth in him.* "Second, I'm paying attention to what they have on. Did they make an effort to dress nice? When you came in, you wore the most horrible brown skirt that was way too big, and your shoes were outdated, but you came in dressed for the job you wanted. If you had been wearing something that looked like a party dress or like you were on your way to a barbeque, I wouldn't have hired you. I'm also following my instincts, but it's all a crapshoot until you hit the one-month mark. People who want to do better show it by coming in on time, doing a good job, and being eager to take on more and grow. Eighty-five percent of the people working here were locked up, and all of them deserved a chance to start over. Many places won't give them that. Society wants you to turn your life around, but when you come home and try to do that, no one wants to see anything but the mistakes you've made. Recidivism is high for that very reason. You've been labeled, and it's hard to remove it. That's why I hire ex-cons and pay them well. I've been where they are, and I know how hard it is."

"That's why everyone working here has your back and works so hard. We do it because you saw past what we were to what we could be. Thanks, boss lady," Maria said with a smile.

Chapter Six

Carla returned the smile. She liked the nickname her staff had given her, even if they didn't know how true it was. She went back to her office. When she first went to work for the company after she was released from prison, Russell, who owned it, offered her an opportunity at getting back on her feet, and it had turned out to be one of the best things to ever happen to her.

He recognized how hard she worked and took her under his wing, teaching her each area of the business. When he told her that he wanted to retire and planned to sell the company, he gave her the opportunity to be the new owner.

Just as she sat down behind her desk, her cell phone rang. "Hey, momma," she answered after checking the number.

"Hey, sugar. How are you?"

"I'm good."

"I called because I'm planning a party for your father's birthday in a few weeks, and I would really like you to come. Even if you can't, I was wondering if Eden or one of your cousins could stay with you if we run out of room around here."

"I'm sorry, momma, I can't."

Her mother was quiet for a minute. "You know, I just don't understand this. You can't let go of the past and just move forward. You act like the people who love you will purposely set you up or something. You have to start trusting people again."

"Why would Eden need a place to stay?"

"I wish the two of you were closer. She moved to Dallas for her new job. Didn't you see her at the engagement party?"

"No. I didn't. If Eden needs to stay with me, that's fine, but no one else."

"Pierson has something to say to you," her mother said quietly.

"Grandma wanted me to tell you about my basketball game on Thursday night in the high school gym," Pierson said when he came on the line.

Grandma wanted you to tell me. Pierson didn't want to tell her anything. It was her mother attempting to fix their relationship. "Do you want me to come?"

There was a long pause. Carla was beginning to think that he had laid the phone down. "It's up to you. You don't have to come." There was some noise as he handed the phone back to her mother.

He doesn't want to have anything to do with me. He never has. "I'll try to be there. I have to go, momma," Carla said, getting off the call before her mother could say anything further.

She closed her eyes and took several deep breaths. Carla wanted to be more involved in Pierson's life, but she stayed away for his own good.

Monster had no idea he had another son, and Carla was determined to keep it that way. So far, neither he nor his mother had figured things out, and one of her children was being raised in a good and positive way.

The only reason for that was that she gave birth to him while in prison, and her mother and father had agreed to take him in. Once she was sentenced, Monster stopped coming to see her.

No one knew who Pierson's father was, but it wouldn't take much for someone to add two and two together and come up with an answer that proved that Pierson's father was Will 'Monster' Johnson.

At least one of her children would have a chance at a life that had nothing to do with drugs and violence. Every time she thought about her daughter and son being raised by Monster's mother, Millie, it burned a hole in her soul. There was nothing she could do about it.

Carla's family didn't even know that Portia and Payne existed. They had no clue that while they had been looking for her, she lived with and married a violent and cruel man. While in prison, Monster handed her children over to his mother to raise. *Millie is the one that should have been called Monster. Evil bitch!*

There was nothing she could do about it now. Her children were eighteen and twenty, and from what she had found out, neither remembered her and believed that she had run off, leaving them when they were four and two. She couldn't control what happened with them, but she would keep Pierson from being raised by the Johnsons if it was the last thing she did.

She toyed with her new necklace. Carla looked at the cufflink she took from Terry and turned it into a pendant. She smiled, looking at the fancy letter W etched into the black onyx stone. *I wonder if Terry figured out that I took it. What would he do if he realized that I had it made into a necklace?* It was the only way she could keep a piece of that night and what she shared with him.

**

Terry couldn't stop thinking about Carla and their night together. He had been so off-kilter by her brashness. "Let's not talk about trivial things. I want to talk about sex," she said to him after they had a few more snakebites.

The look on his face had to be priceless. He was sure he looked as if he was handed a loaded gun but had no clue what to do with it. "That's uh – fine." He nodded.

"Are you single and free to engage in sex without guilt or consequences?"

"Yes," Terry answered, squinting.

"Are you drug and disease free?"

"Yes."

"When was your last aids test?"

"Okay," he said, shaking his head to clear it. "What is this?"

She smiled at him as if she were looking at a cute puppy. "First, I'm going to call you Terry. Terrance is just a mouthful to say." *Especially during sex.* "I want to get a room upstairs and fuck until we collapse from exhaustion. I know that my approach is a little – abrupt and coarse, but I don't have time for bullshit. I need this, and I have chosen you, mainly because I've been told by my cousins that your brothers are great in bed and well endowed. I want to see if it runs in the family, but before we can rock each other's worlds, I need to know that you will not give me any diseases. By the way, I hope you aren't opposed to condoms, 'cause regardless of what you tell me about your medical history, you have to wear one."

Terry glanced around them. *Did I just enter the Twilight Zone? Is she serious?* "Let me get this straight," Terry said, lowering his voice. "You are propositioning me for sex tonight?"

"Yes."

This has got to be some kind of setup. Mike or Carl, maybe. They must have put her up to this expecting me to freak out. Well, let's see how far they plan to take this prank. "Alright. I keep a room here for out-of-town clients. Are you ready to get started now, or should we wait until the party is over?"

Carla smiled seductively. "Eager? I like that, but I think we should stick around for a bit." She looked at her watch. "I'll meet you in the lobby in an hour."

He took his phone from his pocket, handing it to her. "Why don't I just text you the room number?" Terry said, looking at his watch too. "One hour."

Carla entered her number and gave him back his phone. Then she leaned forward and kissed his cheek before walking away. Terry couldn't help but notice how delectable she smelled. As Carla strolled away from him, Terry looked around for his brothers. He expected to find them watching.

To his consternation, Carl was nowhere to be seen. Mike was standing with his arm around Tanya but wasn't interested in what Terry was doing, and Billy was on the dance floor with Betty. His older brother never participated in the hijinks that their younger brothers did.

It didn't change his mind, though. He was sure that his brothers were planning to embarrass him somehow. Terry had to admit that using Carla to do it was genius. He wondered how they got her to go along with their scheme.

Chapter Seven

Terry walked his mother to the entrance where the car and driver he provided for her were waiting. "I had a delightful time," she told him as they crossed the lobby. "I didn't get to speak with Carl, but Mike and Billy's women are splendid. All we need is to find one for you and Carl."

"I'm glad you had a great time tonight," he told her as they stepped outside. He kissed her cheek as the driver held open the rear car door for her.

He waited until they drove away before he went back inside. Terry checked his watch. It was almost time for Carla to meet him. He went to the desk, retrieved a key, and went up to the room. Terry was sure that his brothers would show up shortly.

His brothers used to play pranks on him all the time. They thought Terry was too big for his britches and needed to be brought down a peg or two. Though they had not pulled anything against him in a long time. Carla didn't seem like a woman who would behave so wantonly.

When he first laid eyes on her, he saw maturity and elegance. She was tall and attractive. Carla was well dressed in a stylish gold dress with a vivid green pashmina. She had a great body, filling out her dress with her trim curves. Carla was the kind of woman he needed to go out with. She had a perfect look to compliment him with a touch of the exotic in her golden-brown skin.

He wanted to ask her out, get to know her better, and who knows. *If we liked each other, maybe a year from now I will propose, and we could enjoy the rest of our lives together.* Now he wasn't sure what to think. He knew that he was getting ahead of himself. He didn't know anything about her.

That's what he'd been thinking before Terry removed his jacket, laying it across the back of a chair. Then he walked through the suite. He had never actually stayed there. His administrative assistant had procured the room and made sure that it was ready when they needed it. He was impressed with her selection.

The view of Dallas at night was incredible. Below him, Terry could see millions of lights from businesses and homes twinkling in the darkness. Someone knocked at the door. He crossed the living room space to open the door. *What are my brothers going to do? Have a stripper at the door, or maybe a singing message.*

When he opened the door, Carla entered, putting her purse on the table near the sofa. She tossed her pashmina in the same place as Terry closed the door. "We need to get a few things straight. I'm not interested in an ongoing relationship with you. Once we leave this room, we're done. I know that we'll have to see each other again due to the members of our family being involved with each other, but this is just between us. I want nothing from you but a night of orgasmic delight. Are we clear?"

"Are you – kidding me?" *I know that my brothers had to have put you up to this. This scenario isn't me at all.*

"As serious as a heart attack," Carla said, opening her purse. She pulled out several gold foil packages, holding them up.

Maybe this is real.

"I'm not into anything exceptionally freaky. I'm not interested in oral sex. I have trust issues. I don't do anal, so if that's what you're into, get it out of your mind, and no kissing. I only want your dick. Got it?" She moved away from him into the bedroom, turning on the lights.

This is not a joke. She genuinely wants to have sex. Terry watched as she faced him, reaching behind her back and undid the zipper. Her dress fell to the floor. Then her lacey underclothes joined the dress at her feet. *Good God, Almighty!* Carla was stunning in her nakedness. She was firm, fit, and wickedly wonderful. Terry realized that he was gawking.

She sat on the side of the bed, crossing her legs seductively with a slight smile as Carla crooked her finger, beckoning Terry to come to her.

He moved slowly, but he came when she called, and that was enough to make her grin at him. He stood patiently as Carla undid his belt and the opening of his pants. "Take off your clothes," she ordered, leaning back on her elbows to watch.

Again, he did as he was told, unbuttoning his white shirt. He put his cuff links on the table beside the condom packages Carla had sat there.

She rubbed her thighs together before uncrossing them to allow Terry to look at her, which he did.

Terry watched Carla in amazement. She was unlike anyone he'd ever met. She kept her eyes on him as she touched herself. He took his cock in his hand and stroked it a few times. *Stuff like this only happens in porn. I just met her tonight. After that last drink, I must have hit my head, and I'm unconscious, dreaming all of this.* Dream or not, Terry was going to enjoy it while it lasted. He was tempted to drop to his knees and taste her, but that was on her list of no-nos.

He took one of the condoms from the table and put it on before holding open Carla's legs to climb between them. Terry replaced her hand with his own, looking into her eyes as he rubbed her clit with his thumb. *She's already slick. I guess it doesn't take much to get her going.*

Carla moaned. Reaching up with both hands, she grabbed his shoulders and flipped him onto his back, straddling him. *What the hell? So, you like to be in control? Okay. I can accept that.*

Carla slipped her hand between them. The heat from her hand closing around him burned through the condom. Terry gritted his teeth, hissing as she lowered herself onto his hardness. She closed her eyes, letting air escape from her slightly opened mouth. "Yes!" She said when he filled her.

Carla was still for a few seconds while gripping him within her. *Good guacamole!* He slid his hand up her thighs to her hips. Then she planted her hands on his chest, working her hips, sliding up and down his length. She looked down at him, meeting his gaze. *She's incredible, and that feels so damned good.*

The ways she looked at him made Terry feel as if she were looking at his soul, examining him for his worthiness. Her gaze did not falter. Most people closed their eyes to keep from sharing intense emotions with sexual intimacy. Not, Carla. She wanted everything he had to give in every sense of the word.

He had never been with a woman so acutely aware of her power. It was invigorating. She tossed her head back. "Smack my ass Terry." He obliged. "Harder. I need to feel the sting of it." He hit her again. "Yes, just like that. Again!"

Terry spanked her repeatedly, noting that she picked up her pace. He watched her beautiful brown globes bounce violently. *She felt so delicious sliding against him.* She went wild, grinding and rubbing against him as her orgasm took hold of her body.

Terry rolled her on her back. One of his arms was behind her back with his hand gripping the base of her skull. He used his other hand to cup her knee, holding it, giving him a deeper connection.

Terry never took his eyes from hers as he stroked into her slowly at first and then faster, causing a second wave of pleasure to explode within her. "Yes, Terry, just like that. That's how to make me happy." He continued his pattern of slow strokes and then fast and hard, causing Carla multiple orgasms back-to-back.

He lowered his head, attempting to kiss her. Carla turned her head and pulled at the sheets, breathing heavily. She wanted to close her eyes, but she felt compelled to look at him again. His bluish-grey eyes held her captive.

Terry grunted and groaned, sweat dripping from his brow as he worked to make her cum again. He shifted his body, letting go of her knee, pressing his chest to hers while she wound her legs around him. He attempted again to kiss her lips, but she turned her head.

Carla dug her nails into his back as he kissed and sucked on the side of her neck. "Oh, God!" She said as she let go. Terry continued pounding her until every muscle in his body tightened, and his orgasm erupted. They both trembled and quaked until their bodies relaxed.

Their night together had been beyond incredible, and that was why he couldn't get her out of his mind. Thinking about it made him hard. *It feels like I'm walking around with a baseball bat in my boxers, banging against my legs every time I think of Carla.*

Chapter Eight

Terry stood when he saw his mother coming towards his table. He kissed her cheek. "Mom, you look lovely." Terry held out her chair. When she was settled, he took his seat again.

They looked over the menu in silence for a few minutes. "How are things at the office?" His mother asked, laying the menu down.

"Things are okay. We're having a small shipping issue, but I'll be flying down to Houston tomorrow to see about selecting a new company to solve that. And I've been getting calls from Malcolm Wainright."

"The boy who gave you hell all through school. I hope you're not going to get involved with him. I'm sure he's still a horrible person."

"I have no plans to." There was a brief silence. He knew what was coming next because it was always the same order. His mother would ask about business and then about his personal life.

"Have you met anyone new?"

There it was. *I have, but I can't tell you about it. It might be interesting to see how you react to me having a one-night stand.* "No."

"Do you remember Mrs. Snowden? She lives in the apartment down the hall from me." Terry nodded. "Her daughter has moved back to town. She's a very nice woman."

Terry wasn't surprised by his mother attempting to play matchmaker. Every week that they had dinner together, she brought up his love life and then proceeded to tell him about a woman that would be perfect for him. Terry always went along with it. He would allow his mother to introduce him to this person. Then Terry would go out with them a few times only to discover that she wasn't right for him.

Now that Mike and Billy had found women to be with, he knew that the heat would be on him. His mother would undoubtedly be more determined to match him with someone. *I may as well cut through the usual routine.* "Mother, I appreciate your help, but none of the women you've set me up with are right for me. I think that you should let me find my own future wife."

"If you were any good at it, you wouldn't have married Lindsey, and you wouldn't be divorced now, would you?"

You're right, but I'm not going to tell you that. I'd never hear the end of it. "I really would like not to talk about my failed marriage. Do you do this to Billy?"

"I used to, but now that he's found Betty, I can focus on you."

"What about Carl? He's single."

"When have I ever been able to meddle in Carl's life?" She smiled at him.

His mother had a point. *Carl has always been a tortured soul.* It seemed that his mother was truly focused on him. It might be easier to go along with her for now. "Fine. When am I supposed to meet this woman?"

"Next week. I'll set something informal up and let you know."

After he gave in to his mother, the evening moved along as normal, but Terry's mind wandered back to Carla quite a bit. He would be seeing her again the next day. How would she react to seeing him? Had she even given him a second thought since their rendezvous?

He wanted to call his brothers and find out what they might know about Carla, but he promised her that he would keep their affair private. If he started asking questions about her, they would surely put two and two together and come up with something close to the truth.

Terry had already considered running a background check on her, but that was no way to start a relationship. *She doesn't want that.* He fought his conscious, knowing that even if she didn't want a serious thing with him, he might be able to lure her into something more, using the obvious physical connection they shared.

Her bold behavior wasn't something he was used to, not just in the bedroom but even before that. She was direct and confident, and that was always a turn-on. His only concern was that there was no way for him to gauge her feelings. *I could ask if she has considered something more between us.*

**

After the game started, Carla entered the gym where Pierson's game was held. She kept her sunglasses on and made sure that her hair was covered by her hoodie. Carla didn't want anyone to see her there. She stood beside the edge of the bleachers, glancing into the stands. She could see her mother and father on the other side of the gym, near the back end of the building.

Pierson was on the court. Carla took out her phone and videoed him. *He has skills like his father.* Carla didn't know much about the positions, but her baby was tall and lean and making moves. She could have taken a seat in the stands, but she didn't plan to be there long. She didn't want anyone to see her. There were too many people in Houston who knew her and Monster. Someone was bound to tell him about her being there, which might seem strange to him.

She had just put her phone back in her pocket when she spotted Millie coming towards her. Carla was stunned for a minute. Not because of Millie, but because she was followed closely by Portia. "Fuck!" *Millie being here with Portia could only mean one thing.*

Since Carla had come home, she had only seen her children from a distance. Portia had grown into a beautiful young woman. Carla didn't have much information about them. No one was willing to tell her anything about them. What little she knew about her kids came from Hammer, one of Monster's most dependable men. He had reluctantly given her the information when she ran into him in the grocery store years ago.

Carla turned and exited the gym, rushing to get to her car. *What is she doing here? Does she know about Pierson?*

She was nearly at her car when Millie yelled her name. "Carla!" she kept moving. "I know it's you. You may as well stop."

Carla stopped and took a deep breath before turning to face Millie. She removed her sunglasses and pushed her hoodie off her head. *You've got this; just don't beat her ass when she gets out of pocket.* "Millie," Carla said when the woman got closer. Portia was standing by the door, far enough away that she couldn't hear their conversation.

Millie hadn't changed much. She still wore her hair in a bright red color and wore lashes that belonged on a clown, but then her makeup was applied in the same manner. Her clothes were too tight or too small and clearly inappropriate for a woman her age. "What the fuck are you doing here? Did you think you could sneak in to watch Payne's game, and no one would see you? Even with your little disguise on, I knew it was you the minute you stepped through the door."

Payne? Jesus! Carla had no idea that he played ball. *I should have known.* "Your son has custody, but there is nothing that says I can't be near my child or watch him play a game. I am still his mother."

"Yeah, that's something we can't change. You gave birth to him. I can't deny that, but I raised him, and Portia. I don't want you upsetting their lives. You shouldn't be here.

"The only reason I'm not a part of their lives is because I went to prison for your fucking son! If it weren't for that, I would have raised my children. It was what you wanted all along. I knew it the minute Portia was born. When you held her in the hospital, I could see it in your eyes that you were obsessed. You did everything in your power to get rid of me until I finally got arrested. That was all you needed to get them away from me."

"Bitch, please. You were a crackhead ho who used my son to access the things that meant the most to you, drugs and money. I will never understand to this day why Will loves you. Frankly, I don't care." She stepped closer to Carla. "What I do know is that you better stay away from Payne and Portia or else."

Carla didn't get to say anything else. Portia called out to Millie, "Gigi come on. We're missing the game."

Millie rolled her eyes at Carla. "Stay away from them." Then she turned and walked away.

If my child wasn't watching, I'd snatch that cheap ass wanna be lace front right off yo damned head, and whoop yo ass with it! Carla watched her for a few minutes before getting into her car and leaving. Carla screamed as she drove away. *At least Millie didn't realize that Pierson had anything to do with her. Though how, I don't know. Pierson looks just like Monster.*

Carla wasn't afraid that her parents would know who Payne, Portia, or Millie was. They were a different class of people, but she said a prayer anyway. *Please, Lord, keep any of them from finding out about each other.*

Carla couldn't help but think about how different her life might have been if she hadn't started hanging out with Nelda when her family moved into the house down the street.

Growing up in a very religious environment made Nelda very attractive to Carla as a friend. Nelda's family didn't attend church like most people on their block. Her mother and father allowed their only daughter to do what she pleased most of the time. At least it appeared that way.

The truth was more complicated than that. Her parent's worked multiple jobs, which left Nelda in charge of her life because they trusted her. The first time Carla went to her house after school, she wandered around. It wasn't much different than her home. While she looked around, Nelda disappeared up the stairs.

She returned a few minutes later. "Come to the back yard with me," she said to Carla, who followed her out the back door. They crossed the yard to a shed in the back. Nelda used a key to open it and turned on a light hanging from a cord in the ceiling. "You ever smoked pot?" Carla shook her head. Her father would kill her if she had ever done anything like that. "Well, I do. You can try it if you want."

"My dad wouldn't like it."

Nelda snickered as she took what looked like a tiny pipe and a lighter from behind a turpentine can. "Yeah, I bet. It must be hard being a preacher's kid."

Nelda was right. It was hard. Carla never got invited to parties. Boys wouldn't talk to her. She was fifteen and had never been kissed. "I guess it is," she responded.

"Weed isn't a bad drug. It just mellows you out." Carla watched her carefully as she took a small clear baggie from her pocket. The stuff inside it looked like clumps of dried grass. It had a yellowish tint to it. Nelda took a small piece, putting it into the bowl end of the pipe. She put it to her mouth, flicking the lighter on the bowl end while inhaling.

Carla watched as her new friend sucked the smoke into her body. Then she put the lighter aside, attempting to hand Carla the pipe. Carla shook her head violently. She wasn't going to do that. Nelda finally let out the breath she was holding, allowing some smoke to fill the air. It smelled funny. "Come on, try it. Don't be chicken. I'm not going to tell anyone." Then Nelda coughed. "You are going to love this, I promise. Just one hit. If you don't like it. I'll never ask you to do it again."

Carla licked her lips and pressed them together. She knew it was wrong, but what could it hurt to try it once. She took the pipe, holding it to her lips. Nelda used the lighter, and Carla copied what her friend had done.

"Let it get in your lungs. Don't just hold it in your mouth. Hold it for as long as you can."

Carla did as Nelda told her. When she couldn't hold it any longer, she exhaled and coughed simultaneously. She continued to cough for a while. Nelda laughed. "Yeah, girl! You gonna be good and high now."

That moment led Carla down a long and winding road to where she was now. *If only I had known what my future held, I might have made a different decision. The words 'Just do it once,' got me to try pot, Xanax, dick, and crack.*

Chapter Nine

Carla was glad that the weekend was starting. She was ready to get out of the office and relax. For her, that meant sitting on her sofa with snacks and the remote streaming movies and shows. All she had to do was get through the rest of the day. She had one more appointment with a potential client.

Although her clients could get a quote and schedule the service via the website or phone, a few wanted to further vet the company before agreeing to let 3P handle their shipping needs. This was one of those kinds of clients, it seemed.

Carla's mind had been a tangled mess since her run-in with Millie. She kept expecting Monster to show up at her job or any places she frequented. He had a habit of doing just that.

The entire time she was on probation, she was in a perpetual state of fear and loathing. The man who had done nothing to help her while she was behind bars, who didn't come to see her once, couldn't seem to stay away from her. It had gotten better over the years, but he still popped up occasionally.

He harassed her about renewing their relationship. He threatened her when she let him know that she wasn't interested in being with him again. He was still as bipolar with his feelings as before. Carla only wanted to be free of him. So far, he had not shown up, but that didn't mean that he wasn't planning to or that she wasn't being watched.

She looked down at the onyx pendant on her necklace. Terry was also on her mind. *Obviously, he isn't thinking about you. He has your number, and he hasn't called or sent a text.* Her office phone rang. "Carla Braxton," she answered.

"You're four o'clock appointment is here," Maria told her.

"I'll be right out." Carla replaced the receiver and got up. She moved quickly through the hall to the front office, stopping abruptly when she saw Terry Watson sitting in her waiting area.

He stood, smiling. "Mrs. Baxter, I'm Terry Watson from Technology Revolution." He extended his hand to her.

What is he doing here? I was supposed to meet with Roman Noel. Carla remembered her necklace. She used one hand to make sure that it was inside her shirt. She grabbed his hand and shook it briefly.

"Mr. Watson, it's a pleasure to meet you. Come with me." She turned and led him back to her office. The minute the door was closed, she asked the question dancing in her brain. "Why are you here?"

Terry smiled at her, moving to sit in one of the chairs near the desk while she moved behind it. "I'm here for two reasons. First, I need to hire this company to transport some parts to my factory in

Dallas. I was concerned because the reference we got mentioned that the drivers for your company are mostly ex-convicts. While researching the company, guess whose picture was on the website. Yours. I'm trying to decide if I want to take a shot on this service when I see a picture of the woman who disappeared on me after an unforgettable night."

Unforgettable, huh? "Well," Carla stated, sitting back in her chair. "Before you ask the question, yes, most of my drivers are people who have been to prison. If your concern is whether you can trust the drivers to do their jobs, don't worry. They are trustworthy and dependable or wouldn't be working in this company. If this is more about your company's image, you should look elsewhere."

"Of course, I have concerns about the optics of the situation, but I desperately need to have a service like yours."

I knew it. He's just like Monster, completely concerned with what others think of him. "You said there were two reasons. What is the second reason?"
**

Terry looked her in the eye. "The other reason I'm here is that I wanted to see you again."

He watched her taking in that fact. *Did she almost smile? I can't tell.* It was quick, but Terry swore that he saw her mouth twitch.

"Terry, I told you that we could never have anything beyond that night."

I was hoping you didn't mean it. "You did, but I want to negotiate a new deal."

"A new deal?"

"Yes. Something beneficial to us both."

"In what way?"

"Tell me what you want from me, and I'll tell you what I want from you. Maybe we can come to an agreement that makes us both happy." *Don't shoot me down. Just think about it for a few minutes. Let it marinate and soak in.*

Terry watched her twist and contort her face as she contemplated his offer. He couldn't get over how beautiful Carla was. She wore little to no makeup. She didn't need to; her skin was flawless and even-toned. Her hair was slick, pulled back into a bun at the base of her head. Even in the ugly long-sleeved tee-shirt, crude plaid over-shirt, long khaki pants, and the timberland boots, she looked stylish and classy.

He was so engrossed in his perusal of her that he barely noticed when she answered him. "Before we talk about anything personal, let's get business out of the way unless that was just a ruse to get you here."

"No ruse. The shipping company I've been using can't find drivers, so I've got parts in a warehouse that I need in Dallas yesterday."

"What size shipment are we talking about? Will this be a one-time deal, or are you looking for a permanent replacement to handle all of your shipping needs?"

He smiled. "That depends on how a few test shipments go. I have factories in a few cities, and I have contracts with electronic stores all over the country. This could be a very lucrative deal for your company if you can deliver the goods." He could see the wheels turning in her head. Carla was all about business from the way she looked. Her brow was slightly furrowed, her mouth was set in a thin straight line.

"I can offer you a deal on three test shipments. I would need the pickup and drop-off locations to start with." She took a notepad and pen and slid them across the desk to him. "I'll have one of my salespeople contact you on Monday with the quote. If you agree to it, we'll get started. At the end of the test. You can let me know if you want more."

Terry wrote the information on the pad and pushed it towards her. "Will I be negotiating the final deal with you?"

"No. I'll hand it over to the head of my sales team."

Terry frowned. "That's too bad. I was hoping to make a few personal stipulations."

"That's why the deal will be handled by Bradly," Carla said, grinning at him.

Clever woman. She can see right through me. She knows I'm trying to get back in her pants. "Now, can we talk about my second reason for coming here?"

"No. I only discuss 3P business in this office."

"Can we discuss it tonight, over dinner?"

"No, but I'm willing to discuss it after I let you fuck me in your hotel bed." Carla stood. "Where are you staying?"

I wasn't expecting this, but I like it. Terry stood, watching her as she moved around the desk towards the door. "I'm in the penthouse at the Four Seasons." *That should impress her, but I can't tell from the look on her face. She doesn't look impressed.*

"I'll be there around nine," Carla said as she opened the door. She led him back to the main entrance. "Bradley will be in touch with you early on Monday. Have a delightful evening, Mr. Watson."

"I intend to," Terry said with a smile that took her breath away as he shook Carla's hand.

Chapter Ten

Breathe. Slow. Deep. Just Breathe. Carla stood in the hallway outside Terry's room for a few minutes. After her run-in with Monster at the gas station, she should have gone back home. Though she had been careful and was sure that she hadn't been followed, she didn't want Terry getting mixed up in her problems.

In her excitement to get to Terry, she had been careless when she left her place. Carla didn't check her rearview mirror as she normally did. Carla was pumping gas when she saw Monster's burnt orange Chrysler 300 pulling into the station parking lot. He appeared to be alone, which was odd. He always rolled with a group of thugs. At the very least, Hammer would be with him. He probably was in the car. The windows were too dark for her to see inside at night. Monster got out of the car and came towards her. *Be cool.*

He didn't stop until he was standing inches away from Carla. He let his eyes roam over her as if she still belonged to him. She had dressed for Terry, choosing a clingy red dress in a soft material that stopped just above her knee. "Damn! You still finer than frog's hair, split four ways."

She ignored his old-timey compliment. "What do you want?" Carla asked, facing him.

"Don't play like you don't know. I want you. Same as always. When are you going to quit playing games and come home to big daddy?"

Carla shook her head, looking at the numbers rolling on the pump. Big daddy was what he called his dick. "It's been five years, and you're still asking that question. I'm never coming back. The divorce papers I keep trying to get you to sign should have clued you into that little fact."

"I'll never sign them. When you had my baby girl, I told you we were a family. That ain't gonna change. I meant that shit."

"If we're such a family, why can't I see my kids? Why do they think I took off and left them behind or died? Whatever you have told them is a lie. You don't know the meaning of the word family." Carla took the gas spigot and put it back on the pump.

Monster grabbed her arm, gripping it tight. "Ma told me about you sneaking into Payne's game. I meant what I said. If you don't come home to me, stay away from Portia and Payne. I'm sick of this little independent game you playing. That little funky-ass job you got and that raggedy-ass house don't mean shit. Remember what we had together. You got these people in the streets thinking I ain't shit coz I can't handle you. My boys still cracking jokes about you leaving me. Do you know how many bitches out here want me and what I got? Them years away from me done fucked yo head up. You always thought you was too good, better than everybody else, but you ain't. You was a motherfucking crack-ho, fucking Ronnie and stealing for rock."

There it is, that two-faced switch. "Yeah, but you couldn't get enough of this crack ho pussy, could you?" Carla tried to jerk her arm free of his hold, but it was no use. "Get off me Monster. I keep telling you that I'm not the person I was before prison. I'm not scared of you. You can't control me with fear anymore. You can't hurt me."

He gripped her tighter, jerking her closer. "You think I can't hurt you? Ho, I can always get at you through yo family." Carla's eyes grew large. "That's right, I know who yo momma and daddy is. I know he a preacher. "I wonder if he know all the freaky shit you used to do for a taste back in the day before I cleaned yo ass up." Carla moved her free hand so quickly that Monster didn't see it until it was too late.

Carla pushed the Glock she slid from his inside jacket pocket under his chin, flicking the safety off. She smiled at the surprise and fear in his eyes. He let go of her arm, moving like he would take the gun from her. "Fuck around if you want to. I'll splash yo brains all over my car." The ghetto in her came out. "See, what you forgetting is, that I got nothing to lose. I already been locked up. I can handle living in prison. I have little to no relationship with my kids or family because of you. Blowing yo head off would only set me free. So, you go right ahead and try to take the gun from me if you feeling froggy." He looked into her eyes. "Jump mother fucker. I dare you." She knew that he could see the truth. Monster's hand lowered to his side. Carla backed away from him, moving around the car to the driver's door, opening it. *That's right. I learned some shit while I was locked up. Pickpocketing is one of them.* "Now, I'm gonna tell you this once, and you better remember it. What we were - doesn't exist any longer. We. Are. Done. Stay the fuck away from me! Now, back the fuck away from my car." He didn't move. "Right now!" Carla yelled.

She watched him as he slowly stepped back to the other side of the gas pump. "This ain't over," he said, pointing at her. She could see the man inside the gas station watching them. Hammer finally appeared, stepping out of the car, when he saw the gun in her hand. Luckily there were no other people around them.

"Take yo ass back to the hood where you belong," she said, hopping in the car. She pushed the button for the locks and then the engine, and as soon as it started, she took off.

I really should have gone home, but I'm where I wanted to be. Carla took a deep breath and knocked on the door.

**

It was well after nine when Carla got there. Terry hated to admit it even to himself, but he had been watching the clock for half an hour. He was starting to think that she wasn't coming when she knocked.

He crossed the room. *Breathe, just breathe. She's here now.* He opened the door, smiling. "Hey," he said, stepping aside as she came in. Terry closed the door. Carla sat her purse on the chair as she passed it. She went to the bar. "I was afraid that you had changed your mind about coming." *I shouldn't have told her that. I don't want her to think that I'm some insecure, needy person.*

"So was I," Carla said, pouring whiskey into a glass. "Would you like a drink?"

"Sure," Terry said, moving to the bar. She looked wound up, tight like a clock that won't work. "Wanna talk about what's bothering you?" He asked as she downed the drink and refilled her glass.

"No," she said, pouring his drink. She picked up his glass. He took it. "Cheers," Carla said, touching her glass to his and chugging her second drink. Terry did the same, sitting his glass back on the bar.

Carla came from behind it, grabbing his shirt. She grabbed the edges at the neck and ripped it open, buttons raining down everywhere. She slid her hands up his chest to his shoulders, pushing his shirt down his arms until it landed on the carpet at his feet. Carla undid his belt and pants, shoving her hand into his pants, gripping, and stroking him. *Wow! She's so aggressive. I love it!*

Terry grabbed the fabric of her dress and pulled it up, causing her to stop touching him while he removed her clothing. "Naughty girl," he said, realizing that she was naked beneath her dress.

Carla's hands were back on him in an instant. He stood there, enjoying the feel of her hands stroking him to hardness. When he couldn't take it any longer, Terry kicked off his shoes and stepped out of his pants and boxers. Pushing her hands aside, he picked her up, carrying her to the bedroom.

**

Once she was sure that Terry was sleeping, Carla got out of bed, intending to leave, but she found herself in the living room on her hands and knees, picking up the buttons she ripped from his shirt. When she had them all, she deposited them into her bag. Then she picked up his shirt, bringing it to her nose. *I love his cologne.* She put his shirt on, sniffing the collar.

Carla made another drink and went to sit on the sofa. *Drinking isn't going to help this situation.* She couldn't get Monster's threats out of her mind. While she wasn't as afraid of him as she once was, she didn't want him to do anything to her loved ones. All she wanted was to be free of him and to have some sort of relationship with her children.

She expected him to come after her when she first got out of prison. She figured he would have found out how she had taken money from him. That wasn't what he came for. She should have known that he would be too dumb to realize what she had done. He wanted her back. Why? She had no idea. It wasn't like they had a great relationship to start with.

He spent most of his time chasing paper and fucking around with other women in the streets. Their marriage had always been a farce. He married her so that she wouldn't testify against him if he ever got caught.

She knew all the dirt about his dealings, including where the bodies were buried. She should have never been the one to go to prison. *If his sorry ass hadn't been off fucking some chicken head, I would never have been the one to pick up the drugs that got me in trouble.* The only good thing about the situation was that Carla had been able to stash one of the payments before the cops got to her. If only she had been able to make it to her next drop, she wouldn't have had any drugs on her, and she might have gotten away with more money.

The minute she was bonded out and not being followed, she went to where she had stashed the money. Carla moved it to a more secure location with the rest of the money she had been skimming from Monster.

It was still there ten years later when she was released from prison. *It never crossed Monster's mind that I was the reason the amount in my indictment was less than it should have been. He probably thinks that the crooked police took it.* A part of her believed that the only way to be free of Monster was if he died. *Then I'd only have to deal with his mother.* Carla took a sip from her glass, thinking about the gun in her glove box. She needed to get rid of it. She was positive that it had bodies on it. *I like to add Monster's to it.*

Terry moved like a cat, silently as he crossed the room, sitting on the other sofa, facing her. "What are you doing?"

Chapter Eleven

When he opened his eyes, he thought that Carla had left him like the first time, but she was sitting in the living room wearing his shirt with a drink in her hand. That was incredibly sexy, her in his clothes. She was lost in thought when he sat down across from her. Before she answered his question, she took a sip. "Nothing. Having a drink."

"Are you okay?"

Carla tossed the rest of the drink down her throat and stood. "I'm fine," she said, putting the glass down. She moved around the table. She slipped out of his shirt and straddled him, rubbing herself against him while kissing and licking his neck.

I know what you're doing. Terry fisted her hair, pulled her head back, exposing her throat, and running his tongue down its length. Carla distracted him from asking questions about whatever was bothering her, with sex. He didn't want to stop her, but he wanted to help her if he could. He raised his head, turning her face so he could see her. "Tell me what's wrong. You're sitting out here drinking in the dark. Your mind is anywhere but in this room."

"Right now, my mind is on the dick I'm not getting. Shut up and fuck me already." Carla emphasized what she wanted, reaching between them. She took hold of him, easing herself onto him. Terry couldn't help but moan because she felt so good to him. "Yes, that's what I want, you inside of me." She moved her hips.

He couldn't talk or think with what she was doing to him. His arms locked around her body, one hand still in her hair. He pulled her head towards him to taste her lips. Carla struggled against him. She refused to kiss him, and he was sick of it. He forced her closer until his mouth was on hers.

**

No kissing, please. No kissing! That was too intimate. It was more personal than having all ten inches of him burrowing into her repeatedly. She froze when their lips connected. *If I don't react, he'll stop.* She tried not to, but as he nibbled her lips, she closed her eyes, which was the end of her resistance.

The minute her lids closed, blocking out the image of Terry, it was over for her. Carla opened her mouth to him, allowing him to explore her mouth the same way he had her body. He had cracked that carefully erected wall. She moaned and kissed him back, letting herself float in this new feeling.

They weren't just fucking. This was something else. She tried to consume him through his lips and tongue. It was the thing that she had been trying to avoid. She felt something stirring deep within, and it scared her. *I can't let this happen. I don't want to connect with him like this.*

I can't- "Oh God." *I – I,* "Fuck, I'm gonna cum!" Carla groaned and snatched her mouth from his, pushing her hips forward and arching her back. "Oh, God! Yes!" Her orgasm was stronger and more intense than ever before. Her mind was as fractured as her body as Terry gripped her hips, grinding into her as his orgasm took hold of him.

**

Terry didn't want to let her go, but Carla seemed eager to get off him a few minutes later. He let her go and lay his head back, closing his eyes as she rushed from the room. Cum was still coming out of him. *Lord have mercy on me.* Something had changed when they kissed. He felt it, and he was sure she had too. They connected on a deeper level than she was comfortable with. Deeper than any, he had experienced through sex.

He couldn't move. His bones felt as if they were made of liquid. He might have collapsed if he stood. *We broke the rules, kissing and not* wearing a condom. He wasn't worried about her getting pregnant. Even if she was still fertile, it wouldn't happen. Using the condom was one of her stipulations from the beginning. *We have broken other rules. It was only supposed to be a one-time thing. Now, I want to shatter the rule book she created.*

A few minutes later, Carla came back into the room. Her hair was in place again. She picked up her dress, putting it on. "I have to go," Carla said, looking for her shoes. She went back into the bedroom to get them.

Terry got up, moving to the bar to put on his underwear and pants. Carla came back into the room as he was putting his shoes on. "Wait, we should talk."

"There's nothing to talk about. All of this was a mistake. I don't know what I was thinking."

He didn't want her to leave. Terry tried to think of something, anything. "I'll walk you to your car." It would buy him a few more minutes with her. Maybe he could convince her to talk to him. He realized that he needed a shirt and went to get one from the bedroom. As he pulled one from his garment bag, he heard the door close. He rushed into the living room of the suite. Carla was gone. "Shit!"

By the time he got his shirt on and made it to the door, she stepped into the elevator. There was no way he would catch up to her now. *I'll call her, maybe she'll answer.*

He went back into the room. He grabbed his phone and dialed her number. *Come on, answer. Pick up, damn it.*

"What?" She asked gruffly.

"I said I'd walk you down. Where are you?"

There was a long pause. "Terry, I should never have started this. It was a mistake. I'm sorry. Don't – contact me again." The line went dead. Terry stared at the phone, trying to figure out why she was so determined not to get involved with him.

Chapter Twelve

Leaving Terry was hard, but it was for the best. He was a decent guy, as far as she could tell. He didn't need to get caught up in her messy life. He would get over it and move on. Carla knew that if she thought about Terry, she would think of their kiss and what it meant to her, and she wasn't ready to tackle that. *That's why you ran away like a child. Shame on you.*

As she drove back to her place, Carla checked behind her periodically. She didn't see anything out of the ordinary. *Paranoia, that's all this is. No one is following you.* Monster had stayed away from her for a few months. Carla was pretty sure that the only reason he showed up today was because of her conversation with his mother.

Asking her to come back to him made no sense at all. She knew that it was all about how things looked. Her getting out of prison and not crawling back to him made him look bad. To top it off, she had a good job and a place that belonged to her. She didn't need anything from him, and that's why his boys were making fun of him.

He had always been too concerned with what others thought of him. Carla didn't care. She would kill him before she went back to him. The only thing she wanted from him was a divorce and access to her children. There wasn't a day that she didn't think of Portia and Payne. She wanted to reconnect with them and let them know that they had a little brother. Carla wanted them to know their grandparents, but it didn't seem that she would ever get what she wanted. Not as long as Monster was around.

While she was locked up, she hoped and prayed that he would change. It seemed the only thing that had changed was his waist size. He was no longer the muscled man that he used to be. He was still in decent shape, but his middle was thicker, and his hair was thinner with bits of grey. There was no way that she would have been able to get his gun from him back in the day.

He was slipping in his old age. It was sad that at his age, he was still playing gangster. He would never grow up and do something productive with his life. That was probably because of Millie. His mother thought he hung the moon and stars. *Maybe if she had beat his ass when he was a kid, he'd be a better man today.*

Carla parked in her garage and waited until the door had rolled down before going into the house. She locked the door, deactivated her alarm with the code, and reset it. She walked through the rooms. *No one is here.*

She felt better checking to ensure that no one had been in the house while she was gone. It made her feel safer as she got undressed and showered. When Carla sat in her kitchen with a glass of whiskey later, she didn't feel any better. She was under too much stress. It was times like this that made her long for old habits. *No. we aren't going to think about drugs and how easy life can be when I hit the pipe. I need to call my sponsor right now!*

**

After Carla hung up on him, Terry put his shirt back in his garment bag. He went back to the living room to get the torn shirt but couldn't find it. He also checked around the bar for the buttons that popped off it. They were gone as well. *Why would she take them?*

He fixed himself a drink and sat down. *Carla is tougher than the shell on a Macadamia nut. She won't crack at all.* He nursed his drink as he tried to figure her out. He grabbed his phone from the other room and dialed Roman's number.

"Hello," Roman said, his voice gravelly from sleep.

"Sorry, man, I didn't think about what time it is."

"What's up?"

He could hear Roman moving. He was probably getting out of bed. "Hey, I can call you in the morning."

"No. Tell me what's going on."

Terry gave Roman the facts of his issues with Carla. "I don't know what to do."

"You have to get her to open up to you. It sounds like kissing her broke through a barrier. You have to keep at it until she opens up to you."

"She left and won't answer her phone. I don't know where she lives.

"I can get a background pulled, but that won't happen until Monday."

Terry couldn't wait that long. "I may know a way to get the information faster. Thanks for listening."

"What else am I gonna do? You are my best friend. Call me and let me know how this works out."

"Goodnight," Terry said, ending the call. He hoped he still had Hawk's number on his phone. He didn't want to call his brother to get the number. *Yes! I still have it.* It was late, but he needed this information asap. He hit send and waited. "Hey, Terry? I'm surprised to see your number show up on my caller I.D."

"Hawk, sorry for the late hour."

"You mean early, don't you?"

"Yeah. I need a big, big favor."

"Okay. What is it?"

"You can't tell Carl or Mike about this. I need the address for Carla Baxter in Houston, and I needed it yesterday."

"That's a tall order. It means waking people up."

"I'll pay double if you can get it before noon."

"Triple it, like I said, I'm going to be waking people up for this."

"Deal."

"Call you back in a bit," Hawk said, disconnecting the call. Terry took a deep breath and drank his whiskey.

Chapter Thirteen

"Carla, you look fabulous," Rooster said when she entered his bakery. He came from behind the counter, giving her a brief hug.

"You look great, yourself," Carla said when he released her.

"Would you like something? I just took some banana bread out of the oven."

"Oh, that sounds nice with a cup of coffee."

"Have a seat, and I'll be right back," Rooster said, going back behind the counter.

She was glad that he was so welcoming when she called. Carla thought he might not have remembered her considering how long it had been since she spoke to him. Handling her addiction had felt easy for the most part, but in the last five years, Carla found more days where she struggled than ever before. Even then, she didn't reach out to Rooster.

When she called him, she was afraid that his number may have changed or he wouldn't be available to talk to her, but he was. Rooster invited her to come to the bakery he owned for a face-to-face conversation which surprised her, but she agreed. She was even more surprised that he was working when she called.

Rooster returned with two slices of bread and two coffees. He sat down, taking her servings from the tray and placing them in front of her. "Cream and sugar?"

"Cream only." He called the woman behind the counter, asking her to bring some cream. After the woman delivered it and grabbed the tray, walking away, he said, "How are you really?"

Carla added the cream to her coffee and stirred it. "I'm struggling more right now than ever."

"Why? Has something happened in your life?"

Carla drank from her cup. "Several things, I met a man recently, and things aren't going as I planned them to."

Rooster made a face. "Relationships can't be planned, Carla, you know that."

"Yeah, but I need to be in control, and you know why."

"I remember. What YOU have to remember is that you can't control others. Do I need to recite the serenity prayer?"

"No," Carla replied, breaking off a piece of the banana bread.

"Why are you feeling like you want to use again?" Rooster was getting to the point in a hurry.

Carla ate the piece of bread before answering. "The short answer, escape. My youngest son doesn't want me around. I avoid my family so that I don't have to see and feel his rejection."

"How can you be so sure that what he's projecting is rejection. If I remember your situation correctly, your son doesn't know you. Maybe he's feeling rejected by you not putting in an effort to be around him. What this sounds like to me is not rejection but the fear of it. Weren't you the one who chose not to share what you've been through with anyone? Maybe you need to talk about the details of your past with everyone who loves you. Tell them a little at a time and allow them to ask you questions about what you went through. I bet that helping them understand who you were and who you are now will help ease the desire to lose yourself in drugs."

What he said made sense, but it was easier said than done. "What if you're wrong and they don't want to hear it or try to understand it? Then, what am I supposed to do?"

Rooster took her hand. "The first thing you do is think about all you have accomplished in your sobriety."

I have done a lot. I own a business, my home, I'm debt-free, and I give second chances to people with troubled pasts. I've done a lot with my new life.

"If you still have that feeling, you do what you did today. You call me. I'm your sponsor. I've been there, and I will help you in every way that I can. I know that you don't want to use again, or you wouldn't have called me. One thing that you have to do is stop trying to control everything. For lack of a better way to say it, shit happens. It's how you deal with it that matters, right?" He let her hand go.

"Right," she said, taking another bite of the banana bread. "This is really good."

Rooster smiled. "It was my grandmother's recipe."

They sat there for a while longer. Carla listened to Rooster talk about his bakery and how it came to be. When he got off drugs, baking helped him focus. He baked so much that he had to give away pies and cakes every day. Then someone suggested that he sell them.

"How did you get the name Rooster?"

"I belong to a motorcycle club called Winged Avengers. Everyone in the club has a bird name."

"Yeah, but how did you get your name, specifically?" Carla noticed that his white skin was turning red.

"It's a name based on a sound that I make - occasionally, and I'm not saying anything further on the subject."

Carla giggled. "Okay, but I really want to know now." She respected his desire to keep it a secret. Carla didn't ask anything else. She finished her coffee and bread. Then she thanked him and left.

She felt better after their talk. She did have a control issue. Rooster was right that she had to open up to the people she loved, especially her son.

**

Once she was home, she couldn't sleep. Carla tossed and turned, going over the evening. Terry had taken up residence in her head and wouldn't move out. *It was that damned kiss.* She hadn't kissed anyone in a very long time. She had only kissed Monster once. He wasn't good at it.

On the other hand, Terry was skilled, and that was not a good thing for Carla because now she couldn't get it out of her head. She touched her lips with her fingers in the dark. Sliding them back and forth. *I should have listened to Tanya when she said that there was something different about the Watson men. I thought I only wanted sex, but after kissing him, I want more.* She could never have more of anything as long as Monster believed he owned her.

Carla thought about the gun in her glove box. She should get rid of it, but if she did, she wouldn't have anything to protect herself when Monster came looking for it. Carla knew that he would. If he broke into the house, she could shoot him with it and say it was self-defense. It might be better to have it inside the place, rather than in the car.

She got out of bed and went to get it. When Carla was back in the house, she stood there for a minute. *What was I thinking, taking his gun from him?* Carla wasn't afraid of him. She was more worried that she wouldn't be able to take the life of her children's father out of some sense of preserving the love they had for him.

If it comes down to my life or his, I have to choose mine, no matter what. He is a deplorable human being. I'd be doing the world a favor by ending him. She took a deep breath and went back to the bedroom. Carla put the gun in her panty drawer. She got back in bed and tried to sleep.

**

Music broke through the deep sleep Terry was experiencing. He reached out, fumbling around until his hand landed on his phone. He cracked open his eyes wide enough to see the screen. It was Hawk.

Terry popped up into a sitting position on the sofa as he swiped the screen. "Hawk?"

"I got it."

"Can you text it to me?"

There was a pause, then Hawk spoke. "I got more than her address. I have a complete dossier on her. There's some stuff in here that you should see."

"What kind of stuff?"

"I think it's better if you read it for yourself. I can email it to you. I'd bring it over myself, but I'm not in Dallas."

"Neither am I. I'm in Houston until tomorrow. Can't you just read it to me?"

"Houston? Where in Houston? That's where I am."

"Great. I'm at the Four Seasons Hotel in the Penthouse."

"I can be there in half an hour."

"Okay, see you in half an hour. Triple pay. It is before noon."

"I'll do a wire transfer right now. Is your bank account info the same?"

"Yeah. I'll see you in thirty."

As soon as the line went dead. Terry used his banking app and transferred money to Hawk. He added a thousand dollars as a bonus, making the deposit ten thousand instead of nine. Then he got up, ordered breakfast, and changed his clothes.

Terry had no idea what Hawk could have found that required him to read her file himself. It had to be something horrible, but what? It could be just about anything, but it was big enough that it made Hawk tell him about it.

He tried not to think about it as he answered the door for room service. Just as the man was leaving, Hawk knocked on the door. Terry tipped the staff and welcomed Hawk into the room. "I ordered enough food for two. You hungry?"

"No thank," Hawk said, handing him a large flat envelope. "I wrote the address on the outside, just in case you decide you don't want to know what's in there."

Terry licked his lips, closing his eyes with his hands on his hips. He took a deep breath. He looked at Hawk with his hand out. Hawk handed him the envelope. "Thanks, I sent your money and a bonus." Terry looked at the envelope as Hawk lifted the cover off the food and took a couple bacon strips.

Hawk took a bite, walking to the door. "Good luck, man." Terry watched him leave. Then he looked at the envelope in his hand. He needed to decide and fast.

Chapter Fourteen

She was in the bathroom washing her face when her doorbell rang. Carla rinsed the cleanser off and pat her skin dry. She folded the towel and hung it back in its place. Carla had no idea who could be at her door. She went to her dresser and took Monster's gun with her.

She looked out the side window and didn't recognize the car in her driveway. Carla went to the door and looked out the peephole. *What the hell is he doing here?* Terry was standing on her porch, looking around. *Completely out of place like a turd in a punchbowl.*

Carla went back to the kitchen and put the gun in the junk drawer. Then she turned off the alarm and went back to the door, unlocking it. She opened it and unlocked the glass screen door, pushing it out. "Hi," he said, stepping inside.

Closing the door, Carla looked around to see if anyone was watching. "What are you doing here? How did you find me?" She closed the door, locking it.

"We need to talk." The look on his face was serious. "I'm not leaving until you hear me out."

She pressed her lips together. *I don't know what you want to talk about, but you shouldn't have come here.* "What do you have to say?"

"Can we go to the living room or kitchen?"

Carla didn't say anything, moving past him to the kitchen. *I need a cup of coffee.* She grabbed a mug and K pod and set up the coffee maker. "Would you like a cup?"

"Maybe later," he said, sitting at the kitchen table.

"How did you find me?" She asked, getting another mug and K pod. *It was probably his brother Mike. He had to know people who could do a skip-trace.*

**

"I have friends in high places," Terry told her. He was distracted by the shorts and the tiny tank top that left very little to the imagination. Her back was to him, and for the first time, he saw a bit of a tattoo between the hem of the shirt and the waistband of her shorts. *How did I miss it?* His gaze lowered, taking in her behind and then her lovely thighs. He wanted her. *Focus! Depending on how the conversation goes, I will have plenty of time to find out about the tattoo and explore her captivating curves later.*

She faced him while her coffee brewed. "Why would you just show up at my house?"

"Because you won't answer the phone when I call. I asked my friend to get your address. I know that this thing between us was supposed to be a brief affair with no attachments," he took a deep breath.

"That's not enough. I want us to get to know each other better with our clothes on. Is that such a bad thing?" Terry got up from the table, crossing to her. She looked up into his eyes as he touched her face. "You seem determined to push me away, but something happened when we kissed last night. I know you felt it. There is something between us, something – special." Terry lowered his head to kiss her, but Carla shook her head.

**

Don't kiss him. It'll be the end of life as you know it if you do. Terry didn't give her a chance to move away from him as she intended. He cupped her face, placing his lips against hers. Her lids fluttered closed as her arms circled him. Carla moaned as she opened her mouth to him. *This is what I didn't want. I didn't want to feel like I need him. God help me.*

The kiss was sweet and hot, burning Carla from the inside. Terry lifted her onto the counter. The kiss brought her senses to life, sending fireworks off in her brain and body. She reached between them to touch him, but Terry ripped his lips from hers, stepping back. "Not until we clear the air. You have a habit of distracting me with your voodoo twat."

Carla burst into laughter as she got off the counter. "Voodoo twat?"

"Yes," he said, smiling. "Don't misunderstand. I'm sure that you are wonderful in other ways, but sex has never been like it is with you. I'm completely under your spell."

She made her cup of coffee and added cream before joining him at the table. She was still smiling. What do we need to clear up?"

"I don't want just a sexual relationship with you. I want to wine and dine you. I want to talk to you and have you talk to me, but you have to be willing to participate. Can we try being more than sex partners?"

Carla put her cup down, pressing her lips together as she looked at him. He was serious. *Would he still feel like this if he knew about my past?* "I should tell you something. When you expressed concern about whether you could trust my drivers because they were ex-cons, you never asked if I was one."

"Are you?"

"Yes," she said, meeting his eyes. "I did time for possession and intent to distribute." She waited for him to take it in, react, and tell her that he didn't want to see her again.

"You know my brother Carl went to prison for something similar. He learned his lesson and moved on with his life. It seems that you've done the same. I can't hold your past against you. We all make mistakes, some worse than others. I'm concerned with your present – and your future."

"Do you mean that? I may not know you well, but I feel that your image is important to you. I don't want my past to cause problems for you."

"Why would it. It's not like we're going to go into a restaurant announcing that you went to prison years ago, right?"

Carla took a deep breath. *I want to believe you, but it's hard to trust anyone after all I've been through.* "No, but what happens if some business associate of yours learns about my past, affecting your business?"

"That could happen, but I'm not letting that keep us from exploring what's between us." He paused, looking at her. "So, are we going to try having a real relationship?"

"I'm not sure that I know how to. My previous relationship was anything but normal."

Terry got up from his chair, taking her hand. He pulled her up and into his arms. "We'll figure it out together," he said before kissing her.

It will work out fine. He's not from around here. Even if we are seen together in public, no one would ever suspect me of dating someone like Terry. I'll do all I can to keep Monster away from him. The same way I look out for everyone else.

Chapter Fifteen

Terry should have told her about the envelope containing her background check, but he hadn't opened it. He decided that whatever was in it wasn't worth the distrust it would cause if he mentioned it to Carla. He had stuffed it into the bottom of his briefcase, and he had no intention of opening it.

You may have secrets, but they are yours until you share them with me. "Let's have lunch. We can go anywhere you want."

"I'd rather stay here if that's okay with you. I usually spend my Saturdays vegging out on the sofa with food while binge-watching my favorite shows."

"That sounds great."

"If you were at home, what would you be doing today?"

"Thinking about you," he said, watching her move around the kitchen, gathering food to put on a tray.

"Other than that?"

"Probably working or possibly at the country club playing tennis or golf. Do you play?"

"Yeah, table tennis and miniature golf," Carla giggled.

"I'd be happy to pay for lessons if you want to learn to play tennis or golf. It would be fun if we could play together when you come to Dallas."

"Thanks, but I'm not exactly the tennis type. I'd prefer something like softball."

"Do you enjoy watching baseball? I have a box at Rangers stadium. We could watch a game sometime."

Carla picked up the tray of snacks to take to the living room, but Terry took it from her. "Thank you," she said, leading him to the living room. "You know that you don't have to do that."

"Do what?"

"Brag. You tend to highlight your accomplishments and what you have. I don't care about any of that. It doesn't matter to me what you have. I want to know you, the real you." Carla picked up the remote and handed it to Terry after he set the tray on the coffee table. "You pick something while I get the drinks. Would you like liquor, beer, or a soft drink?"

"I'll have whatever you're having." Terry sat down on the sofa with the remote, looking through the streaming options. He rarely watched shows or movies. He wasn't sure what to pick. Terry was still scrolling when Carla returned, sitting down two Heinekens on wooden coasters. He handed the remote over. "You decide."

**

"You don't watch much TV, do you?" Terry took a sip from his beer, shaking his head. Carla turned off the monitor. "Why don't we just talk then, get to know each other better?"

"Alright," Terry said, grabbing a chip from the platter on the table. "Tell me about the tattoo on your lower back."

"Not much to tell. I got it a long time ago before realizing that my body was a temple." Carla hated the tattoo. She could have gotten it removed. Some lasers would break it down and eliminate it from her body, but she kept it to remind her what she would never do again.

"Show it to me."

Carla turned, lifting her shirt. Terry's fingers were cool against her skin as he touched it. He slid his finger into her shorts, pulling them down a bit. "August seventeen, nineteen ninety-nine. What's the date for? Is that when you went to prison."

Carla turned to face him. *Do I tell him the truth?* Since the image was of a pair of handcuffs, it made sense that he would assume it had to do with her prison record. *Tell him the truth.* It was a test, one that she hoped he would pass. "No. That's the day that I got married. We got matching tattoos."

"You were married? For how long?"

Carla took a deep breath. "Not were. Am. He refuses to sign the final papers. I have continuously refiled, but he won't let it be over. That's part of why I only wanted a physical relationship with you. The last time I got involved with someone, Monster beat him up. I didn't want to take the chance that he would hurt anyone else. Because of that, it will probably be best if we only go out in public in Dallas. I don't want anything to happen to you."

**

"You're still married to – Monster, who beat up the last man you dated. You want us to hide our relationship?" Carla made a face and nodded her head. "Well, I'm not afraid of Monster, and maybe if he sees that you have truly moved on, he'll be more willing to accept that your marriage is over." Carla shook her head. "Why are you looking at me as if I have two heads?"

"Because you are insane. I just told you my ex's name is Monster, and he beat up the last guy I got busy with, and you are calm, cool, and collected, sounding very rational about him coming to grips with the fact that I've moved on."

"If you expected me to go running back to Dallas, I won't. Now, if you need me to talk to this guy for you – "

"Oh hell no!" Carla said, grabbing his hand. "You stay out of this and let me handle Monster, okay?"

He could see that she was very serious. Though, she had no reason to be afraid on his behalf. He could handle Monster. "Why do they call him that?"

Carla shook her head again. "Nope, we are done talking about me. It's your turn. Tell me something about your life."

Terry held on to her hand, pulling her closer. She nestled into his side. *I like how she fits perfectly there.* "There's not much to tell about my life. I work most of the time. I have dinner every Thursday night with my mother. At this dinner, she proceeds to play matchmaker and introduce me to the kind of woman she thinks I need."

"Aw, that's cute."

"Cute? It's a pain. Thanks to Tanya and Betty, she only has me to focus on."

"What about Carl?"

"She would never try to set him up. He wouldn't stand for it. On the other hand, I'd do almost anything to make her happy."

"Even marrying the wrong woman?"

"I already did that, and it had nothing to do with my mother. Her name was Lindsey. She was only interested in my money."

"That's horrible. How long were you married?"

"Three years."

"What made you split up?"

"There are a few reasons, but one was she didn't like my mother very much. She was also determined to get pregnant. I thought that she simply wanted to be a mother, but then I heard her on the phone with a friend saying that it was the only way she could be sure to get extra money when she divorced me. She was willing to have kids just to get child support payments and alimony. That's when I realized that she never loved me at all. The joke would have been on her, though. I had a vasectomy in my late thirties. I've never wanted children."

"Really? Why not?"

I hate kids. "I'm just not the kid having type. I was in my late forties during my marriage. I'm too old for parenthood."

"Is that so? How about making out? Are you too old for that?" Carla grabbed his shirt and pulled him down for a kiss. He forgot about the hurt Lindsey caused and focused on the pleasure Carla gave him.

Chapter Sixteen

As they inched closer to the valet stand in front of the restaurant, Carla turned to Terry. "I really think that we should get something to go and take it back to the house." She didn't want Monster doing anything to Terry.

"Sweetie, relax. I promise you that everything will be alright," Terry said as he stopped, and their doors were opened by the attendants.

She was feeling paranoid that somehow, they would come in contact with Monster. *You're not concerned because you've probably never had to deal with someone like my ex.* Carla shook her head and got out of the car. Terry came around to her side and took her hand, leading her into the building. Fortunately, there wasn't a long wait. She couldn't help herself; Carla glanced around the restaurant looking for familiar faces.

Even after they were seated, she kept her eyes on the door. Terry grabbed her hand after the waiter had taken their order. "You have to relax. Everything is fine."

"You just don't understand how evil he can be."

"Explain it to me then."

I don't want to. I really don't. "It's not something we should discuss in public, especially while eating." Just thinking about some of the things she'd witnessed made her feel sick.

"Okay," Terry said, giving her hand a squeeze. "Then, tell me about how you ended up at 3P."

She wasn't sure that he would be interested in how shitty life could be for someone who had just gotten out of prison, but he asked, so she told him. "When I got out, I needed to find a job that paid well enough to fight –" *Should I tell him. He said he doesn't like kids.* "I needed money to get custody of my children from him. They were living with his mother when I came home. I knew that it would be a huge fight. I expected to get a divorce and custody of my children, but that hasn't happened. The man who owned HT Shipping gave me a job driving locally for him. He understood my situation. He wanted to help, and driving would pave the way for me to make the kind of money I might need. After realizing that I was fighting a battle I would never win, he put me on long-haul jobs. Eventually, he gave me a job in the office. He taught me everything about the business. Then he sold it."

"The new owner kept you on after the sale. It's great that they saw how valuable you were to the company."

**

During dinner, Carla asked many questions about his business and how he got started. Her interest was genuine. She asked many questions, not just about how well his company was doing but also about how new product ideas were generated.

Their conversation shifted again and again until Terry found himself telling her about his childhood and what it was like growing up with three brothers. "It was interesting growing up with them. Billy and I are very close in comparison to Mike and me. The age gap between us is pretty big. Also, Billy and I were more scholarly. I was into science and math. Billy preferred literature and history."

"What about Carl and Mike? What were they into?"

"With Carl, it's hard to say what he liked in school. He tended to disrupt things quite a bit. We found out in his teen years that he was handy with tools and things like that. He liked to help our father fix things around the house. Mike was good at everything, but he excelled at sports. He played football, baseball and was on the wrestling team."

"How did you all get along? I can't imagine four boys around the same age not fighting and causing your parents trouble."

"Well, I went to boarding school when I was about ten. So, I wasn't there with them most of the time. Though summer breaks could be tough. Mike started a lot of scuffles between Carl and me. He was pretty slick about it. We'd be punished while he got treated like a good boy," Terry laughed.

"Why did you go to boarding school and the others didn't?"

"A few of my teachers realized that I was exceptionally smart and had my mother test my I.Q. When they found out how smart I was they petitioned to get me into a school for children who excelled in math and science. I got in with a fully paid scholarship. What was it like for you growing up with your sister?"

Carla wiped her mouth, swallowing her steak. "We didn't spend much time together. I was twelve when she was born. I was well into my rebellious stage when she was out of diapers, and I was living on my own shortly after that."

"So, you two aren't close?"

"Not really. We see each other from time to time, but We're very different people. She was a good girl and kept her distance from me."

"That's a shame," Terry said, signaling the waiter for the bill. "Well, you're both grown now. You should get to know each other. Nothing is more important than family."

Chapter Seventeen

On the ride back to Carla's house, they talked about their taste in music. She told Terry that she liked jazz, pop, and Country music. "Country, you actually like country music?"

"Yes, why is that so hard to believe. I admit that I probably would never have given it a chance if it weren't for one of my bunkies, Cassi Lynn. She played it all the time. It grew on me." Carla's phone rang.

Terry turned down the radio as she took the call. "Hello," she said to whoever was on the phone. "Is everything alright?" The person on the other end continued speaking. Terry could hear them talking but couldn't make out what was being said. "Well, congratulations," Carla said, smiling. "Don't worry about it. I'll talk to Bowleg myself." She was quiet for a minute. "Absolutely not. You stay with your wife." The man on the other end said something else to Carla that made her frown. Then she said. "Put her on the phone. Don't worry." There was a brief break before Carla spoke again. "Senora Hernandez, nose preocupe. Angel no va a perder su trabajo. Se que acaba deempezar, pero deberia estar con su esposa y el bebe. El no va a ser despedido. Prometo." A female speaking in Spanish said something. "Si soy su jefa." *I wouldn't know that she wasn't Hispanic if I closed my eyes.* The woman said thank you in English and Spanish. It was the only thing he understood. "No tienes que agradecerme. Es lo correcto. Felicitaciones por el nuevo bebe. Buenas Noches." Carla disconnected and dialed someone else. "Hey, it's Carla. I just spoke with Angel Hernandez. His wife went into labor earlier." She paused as the other person spoke. "Yeah, I know she's way early. I told him that I'd call you so that you could get someone to cover his shift."

They talked for a while about the situation. Carla's employee hadn't been working for her long, and his mother was scared that he would lose his job. Carla spoke to her, assuring her that Angel wouldn't.

Terry was pulling into her driveway when she finished her call. He was staring at her with a big smile. "You're awesome. I had no idea that you spoke Spanish and so well. Did you learn in school?"

"Yeah, the school of hard knocks," Carla said with a snort, getting out of the car. "I learned it because I had to. We live close to Mexico. There are a lot of Spanish-speaking immigrants here, and many don't know English."

She made it sound like it wasn't a big deal. Terry had learned French in school, and it had not been easy for him. He could barely recall any of it, let alone speak it so well. *It kind of turns me on to think of her speaking another language.*

As soon as the alarm was turned off and the door was locked, Terry kissed her. She was surprised and made a squeaking noise when he pushed her against the wall, pressing himself against her body. Carla dropped her purse on the floor, sliding her hands up his back as he nibbled and sucked her lips.

He loved the moaning sound she made and wanted to hear more of it. He took his mouth from hers. "I'm ready for dessert," he said, grabbing her hand, taking her to the bedroom. *I'm going to spread you across the bed and devour you.*

Earlier in the day, they had only kissed and caressed each other. Terry was ready to do some of the things that had been off-limits because of Carla's no-strings-attached list of rules. All bets were off, and Terry intended to enjoy himself, especially since he had to leave the next day. *I want you thinking about me as much as I think about you.*

Carla turned on the lamp by the bed. Terry removed his jacket, but before getting much further, Carla came to him, grabbing his tie. She yanked on it, making him lean down close to her.

Her tongue flicked out, licking his lips before she kissed him, wrapping her arms around his neck. He gripped her butt, sliding his hands down her legs. Then he lifted her, placing her thighs along his hips. Terry wanted her to feel how hard he was for her.

She gasped, lifting her mouth from his, as his hardness rubbed against her. Carla smiled and continued kissing him, locking her legs around his waist. He carried her to the bed, taking her hands from around his neck once they lay on it.

Terry held her hands above her head, continuing to kiss her for a while. When he lifted his mouth from hers, she said. "I like the way you taste."

"I can't wait to taste these lips," he said, letting go of one of her hands to touch her between her legs. Carla shook her head. Her entire body grew tense and rigid. "What?"

"I told you I wasn't into that."

"I didn't think you meant me going down on you. I assumed you meant that you don't like giving head. Why don't you like it?"

Carla pressed her lips together and closed her eyes. "I've never done that before."

Terry got up, looking down at her. "Are you serious? How can that be?"

Carla sat up. "Monster didn't do that. He said it nasty."

"What about other men that you've been with?"

"There were only two others, and we just fucked."

Terry believed her, but it was hard to fathom how this Monster could be so selfish. He was pretty sure that Carla had gone down on him. She deserved to be please in any and all ways possible.

Terry held out his hand to her, pulling her to her feet. She had been so aggressive with him before. *I wonder if you feel the need to be in control because you had none with him.*

He brushed his lips against hers. She relaxed, kissing him back. When he pulled back, he looked into her eyes. "I want to please you with every part of my body. I intend to show you that licking and tasting you is not nasty. It will give me only a small

portion of the pleasure I intend to give you tonight."
Terry let go of her hands, grabbing the hem of her
dress, pulling it over her head.

He tossed it aside before removing her
undergarments. Terry kissed her mouth again. Then
he began his exploration of her body with his lips,
starting along her jawline and working his way down
her body, slowly and methodically. Every sound and
catch in her breath brought him joy.

Chapter Eighteen

By the time Terry was on his knees, placing kisses along her lower stomach, Carla was dripping wet. He pushed her back until she was on the bed. Spreading her legs, he kissed her hip, then the tops of her thighs working his way to the center.

Carla held her breath as he crossed over to the other side repeating his process. When he returned to the juncture, Terry pushed his face forward, inhaling. He slid his shoulders under the back of her legs, splaying his hands along her sides, urging her to lay down. Carla did as he directed.

His warm breath tickled the damp skin of her coochie. Then she felt the tickle of his thin mustache against her shaved skin. She gasped loudly at the first swipe of his tongue against her clit. She could feel the smile just before his lips latched onto her, and he sucked. "Oh, Jesus," she said, pressing her hands into the bed.

Terry alternated between licking and sucking, with Carla grabbing the covers and yanking as she got nearer to her release. What he was doing felt so lovely, but the feeling grew exponentially when he inserted his finger inside her and pressed.

Carla was close to exploding. Her hands were suddenly in his hair, gripping his head as she squirmed against his mouth and hand. He changed his tactic when she thought she would cum, allaying her orgasm. Then he would start the process again, only to halt her release. She gripped his head with both hands and worked her hips furiously, determined to make him finish the job. "Terry, baby, make me cum. I want to cum so bad. Please, baby."

He replaced his tongue with his thumb, putting pressure on her clit and G-spot. Carla closed her eyes arching her back. "Oh, God!" She yelled as she let go. Fluid gushed from her. Carla was so caught up in what was happening to her that she was unaware of Terry getting to his feet for a minute.

He was nearly undressed when she calmed enough to look at him. Her lower body and thighs were soaked. *I need to get up, but I'm so shook by what he just made me do. I've heard people talking about squirting, but I never believed it was real. That's what that was. I know it. How did he make me do that?*

He returned to her when he was naked, entering her as he leaned forward, kissing her between words. "See." Kiss. "How." Kiss. "Delicious." Kiss. "You." Kiss. "Are." Carla said nothing. She continued kissing him as she gripped the back of his head with one hand and his ass with the other, letting him bring her more and more pleasure.

**

Carla was sipping coffee and looking out the kitchen window when Terry came in. She couldn't get over how special the night before had been. Terry showed her over and over that he liked oral sex. Carla had been deprived of many things while entangled with Monster. Sexual pleasure was definitely on that list. Even during intercourse, he didn't always please her. *Rarely would be more to the truth.* "Morning," Terry said, putting his arms around her waist, kissing the back of her neck.

She pushed Monster from her mind. "I disagree with you about something you said last night."

"What?"

Carla sat her mug down, turning to face him. "What you did, going down on me,mo it was nasty. Good nasty." She giggled and wrapped her arms around him.

Terry laughed too. "Good nasty, huh? You were kind of nasty yourself," he said, referring to her reciprocation later in the night. He kissed the tip of her forehead, the end of her nose, and then her lips. He sighed heavily when he took his lips from hers. "I don't want to leave you today." Carla sighed too. She didn't want him to go. "Can you get away next weekend?"

"I'm sure I can work something out."

"Good, I'll send the plane for you on Friday."

Carla rolled her eyes. "You don't have to do that."

"What good is it to have a plane, if I don't fly my woman in for a weekend of romance and debauchery? I'm not trying to show off. I just want to make the trip easy for you. Besides, I thought we could join the mile-high club on the way back to Dallas."

Carla smiled, nodding her head. "Alright."

"Walk me to the door. I still need to pack and check out of the hotel." He held her hand as they walked to the door. "What are you going to do today?"

"I'll be late, but I'm going to church. After that, I'll come home and wash the two sets of sheets that we've messed up. I still can't believe that you made me do that twice." *Who would have ever thought that I was a squirter?*

At the door, Terry kissed her slowly, thoroughly. "See you Friday. I'll call you later tonight, okay?" Carla nodded with a smile as she let him out. She watched him until he was driving away. *Tanya warned me. I should have listened because now I'm hooked on that man.*

Chapter Nineteen

Carla eased through the door of the gallery of the church. She quickly found a seat among the people who chose to sit there instead of on the main floor. Carla always sat in this area because it gave her a better view of her father as he gave his sermon and her mother and Pierson, who sat in the first and second row of the sanctuary.

She believed that they would be embarrassed by her presence. Carla was certain that her father's congregation knew her drug and criminal issues. Carla felt that she had done enough to cause her family pain. It was better if she stayed hidden.

She couldn't recall the exact date, but sometime during her third year in prison, she picked up a bible that belonged to her bunkie and started reading. All of the things that her father had taught her about God and the Gospel came back. Over time it strengthened her and allowed her to see that God still loved her, that she could get her life together.

One of the things she did while locked up was to get her GED. She never talked about it to anyone in her family. As far as they knew, she was still a high school dropout. They probably believed that her soul would never be redeemed, that she had never repented for her sins, but she had. She thought that God had forgiven her.

She could see her father fairly well from her seat as he moved to the lectern to give his sermon. She had been coming to church every Sunday since her return to the world. Carla would listen to the speech and leave before church let out to avoid contact with anyone who might recognize her.

Her father's voice filled her ears and mind. "Good morning, family. It is a glorious Sunday. Praise the Lord."

"Amen," the congregation said.

"First John, chapter three, verse eighteen says: Little children, let's not love with words or speech but with actions and truth." Her father looked around his flock before continuing. "God was telling us that talk is cheap when it comes to love. In this verse, he was saying, put up or shut up. You can say that you love someone, but it means nothing if you don't prove it with actions. A mother can tell her child, I love you, but it means nothing if she won't feed him when he's hungry. The action must accompany the words. If you're married and you say I love you to your spouse, but you go out and have an affair, you may as well have kept those words to yourself."

Carla listened carefully, feeling that there was a connection between her father's words and her life. She loved her family, but she never showed that love in a tangible way. She hid in the back of the church; she watched her son play ball without letting him see or hear her cheering for him. Carla needed to put up or shut up. It wasn't just about Pierson, though. She needed to do the same thing in all facets of her life. That's the lesson she got from the sermon.

Instead of sneaking out of church before the service ended, she stayed. Carla didn't go down to shake her father's hand or hug her mother, but she didn't try to fade into the background either. It was just a small step, but it was something for her to be proud of.

**

Carla stopped to pick up a few things from the grocery store on her way home. She was looking at the produce when Monster appeared next to her. "Don't you look nice this fine Sunday afternoon?"

I just can't catch a break. Carla pushed her buggy around, trying to move away from him. "What? You not gonna talk to your husband? Going to church don't erase all the shit you did, stealing and dealing. You can't wash that away, baby."

Carla knew that he chose this moment to fuck with her because they were in public. He strolled behind her. "I know about your little white boyfriend. I know that white dick ain't hitting you right."

How did he know about Terry? "My sex life isn't any of your business."

He moved around her, making her stop to keep from hitting him. "Everything about you is my business, and it always will be."

Carla closed her eyes. She didn't want to cause a scene in the grocery store. She counted to calm herself. *One, two, three, four, five, six, seven, eight, nine, ten.* "Will, I don't understand why you do this.

You have a dozen women who love being involved with you. Why do you continue to do this? I just want to end it."

"You belong to me."

"I am not a car or diamond watch. You don't own me, and I'm never coming back to you. Just let me go."

"I can't. I want to, but I can't. I want you back."

"No."

He shook his head. "Tell the white guy at the bakery that I'll fuck him up if I catch you two together." Monster turned and walked away.

He's talking about Rooster. He doesn't know anything about Terry. Thank God. Her relief turned to remorse when she thought of Monster hurting her sponsor by mistake.

**

Carla was still thinking about her father's words hours later. She wished that it were as easy as he made it sound. Carla believed that she was showing love for her children and her parents by staying away from them.

It wasn't fair to her to do so. She didn't get to hug them or laugh with them. Carla wanted her children to get to know each other and spend time together, but that couldn't happen with things the way they were. Something needed to change.

Carla was in the kitchen cooking dinner when her cell phone rang. It was her cousin, Betty. "Hello," she sang, putting the call on speaker.

"Well, don't you sound happy."

"I am happy, I guess. How are you this lovely Sunday afternoon?"

"I'm good. Have you been drinking?"

"Not yet. I'm just in a good mood," Carla said, stirring her sauce.

"I'm happy to hear that. I'm calling to invite you to come to visit next weekend. Billy and I were talking, and we thought that we should get both sides of our families together for a barbeque or something so everyone could get to know each other better. I invited your parents and Pierson. They haven't said they'll come, but maybe you all can come together. Are things getting any better between you and him?"

Carla blew air out of her mouth and turned the fire off. "Not really, but it will get better, I'm sure." She would be in Dallas, but her plan was to spend that time with her new man. *I'm not ready to tell her about me and Terry.* "I have plans already for next weekend."

"Can you change them?"

"I'll see what I can do. No promises, though."

"Okay. Aunt Shelia said she's throwing a big house party for your dad's birthday, so I'll see you there if I don't see you this weekend. I know that you won't miss that. Seventy-five is a big deal."

"It is."

"Alright. I have to go. I hope you'll come."

"I'll let you know if I change my mind," Carla added. Love ya."

**

The first thing Terry did when he got to work on Monday was go to Roman's office. They were alike in many ways, coming into the office earlier than most. Roman's door was open, and music was playing when Terry stepped inside. "Good morning."

"Hey there," Roman said, looking up from his computer. "How did things go with your lady?"

Terry smiled as he took the chair in front of the desk. "Quite well."

"So, you got laid?"

"I don't kiss and tell," Terry said, still smiling.

"You don't have to. The look on your ugly mug gives it all away. I take it that this wasn't just a one-time thing."

"No, it wasn't. In fact, I will be unreachable this weekend. As much as I like this, I didn't come in here to talk about my woman. I came to tell you that we should negotiate a long-term deal for all of our shipping needs with 3P if the test runs work out well."

Roman leaned back in his chair. "You really did have a great weekend."

Terry didn't make any further comments. He got up. "I'll see you at the ten o'clock meeting."

On his way back to his office, Terry thought about his phone call with Carla after he got home. He could hear the happiness in her voice when she answered. "Are you home safe and sound?" She didn't bother with simple greetings.

"I am, and I miss you like crazy."

"Is that so?"

"Yes. I'm tempted to get back on the plane and fly back to Houston."

"What about work? Wouldn't they miss you?"

"I doubt it. Besides, I could do what I do just about anywhere on earth. The only problem is that if I came back to you, I don't think I'd want to work very much."

"That's too bad because I have a job that would be perfect for you. It requires skill and stamina. You'd have to have incredible oral skills, and you need to be good with your hands."

By the time he got off the phone with Carla, he was rock hard and hated that they lived so far apart. He would see her in a few days. Then he could do all that they discussed.

Chapter Twenty

Her work week started the same as always, but things changed on Tuesday. Halfway through her second cup of coffee, Carla's mother called her. "Momma, what's going on?" *I hope everyone is okay.*

"Hi, sugar. I needed to speak to you about your plans for this weekend. Betty said that she invited you to a gathering at her house. Were you planning to go?"

"I don't know. She said she invited you and daddy too."

"She did, but your father and I have decided not to go. We are planning a little getaway to Padre Island. This would be a perfect time for you and Pierson to spend time together."

Carla was quiet for a minute. *Put up or shut up time.* "You know what, Mom. It sounds perfect."

"It does?" Her mother sounded surprised.

"Yes. I'll figure out my travel plans and call you back tomorrow and tell you when I can come get him on Friday."

"Alright. I'll tell Pierson when he gets in from school. Bye sugar."

"Bye momma." Carla ended the call and lay her phone on the desk. *I'll have to call Terry and reschedule our weekend.* She knew that he would be disappointed, but he would get over it. She'd been thinking about what her father said on Sunday. She loved her son, and she needed him to know that. Spending the weekend with him was a start at healing the rift between them.

Her desk phone buzzed. It was Maria. "Yes ma'am," she said, answering the blinking line.

"There's a young lady here to see you."

I don't have any interviews today. "Who is it?"

"Portia Johnson."

I know she didn't just say my daughter's name. "Did you say, Portia Johnson?"

"Yes."

"I'll be right out," Carla told her, replacing the receiver. *What in the world is happening?* She had no clue why her child would be at her office or how she knew where she worked. Carla walked down the hall swiftly, freezing when she got to the waiting room.

As sure as the sun rose in the east, her daughter was there. Carla looked around, wondering when and where Millie or Monster would pop out. *Would they use her to get to me?* That was the only way she could imagine her daughter knowing where to find her.

She took a deep breath, trying to calm her nerves. "Portia?"

Her daughter stood, giving her a small smile. "Momma."

Carla's heart danced in her chest. In all the time since she'd been home, she hadn't been close enough to her kids for them to really see her, but her daughter recognized her. She rushed across the room, embracing her daughter. She squeezed her tight, muttering over and over. "I can't believe you're here. God, is this really happening?"

She soon realized that they were both crying. Carla rubbed her back. "Oh my, baby girl. It's so good to hold you in my arms."

When they finally loosened their hold on one another, Carla looked into Portia's eyes. "What are you doing here? Where's your father and Millie? Do they know you're here?"

Portia shook her head. "No."

"Come with me," Carla said, taking her hand, leading her back to her office. She couldn't believe that she was actually touching her baby.

As soon as the door closed behind them. They hugged again. "I knew it was you when I saw you at Payne's game." Carla pulled away from her, touching her face.

"Here, sit down," Carla said, moving the chairs in front of her desk to face each other. She held both her hands, still testing to ensure she wasn't dreaming.

"I asked grandma who you were. She wouldn't tell me. I knew it was you. I told Payne, but he didn't believe me. Grandma always told us that you left because you didn't love us. I knew it wasn't true. I remember you reading us to sleep and all the kisses and hugs. I didn't forget you."

Carla let go of one hand to wipe at Portia's tears. "I didn't leave you by choice. I had to go away, and they wouldn't let me see you or your brother when I came back. I would never have left you."

"I know."

"How did you find me?"

"I snapped a picture of you talking to Grandma at the gym. Then I asked Hammer if he knew where you were. He didn't want to tell me, but he finally did."

"If he knows, then your father will know," Carla said, fear pushing aside her joy.

Portia shook her head. "No, he won't tell him. He and daddy have been fighting a lot, and I know a secret about Hammer that he doesn't want daddy to know. He'll keep my secret as long as I keep his."

"Don't be so sure about that." *I used to think Hammer was on my side too, but I was wrong.*

"It doesn't matter. I'm twenty years old. I can do what I want."

"You don't know your father and grandmother as well as I do. They can be dangerous. You need to be very careful with them, especially about seeing me. Do you understand?"

Portia nodded, looking at their joined hands. I'm not going to let them come between us, but I won't tell them until you think it's okay."

Carla thought about it for a minute. "Don't tell your brother. Not yet. I know that he's old enough to make his own decisions, but your grandmother can be very controlling."

"Okay," her daughter said, nodding her head. "What happened to you? Why did you leave?"

Carla hated talking about her past, but it seemed that everything that she had kept in the closet was desperately trying to get out. *The truth shall set you free.* Carla squeezed her child's hands and told her everything from the day she went away to that moment of seeing her in the reception area.

Chapter Twenty-One

Carla hated to see Portia drive away. She almost started crying again. Then she realized that they would see each other again soon. Despite loving her grandmother and father, Portia was a bright young woman. She had a cosmetology license and was working to open her own shop. She took business classes at the local college and chose that over going to a university to stay close to her brother.

Portia expressed concern about how close Payne was to Monster. She believed that he idolized his father and wanted to be like him. Portia tried to keep him grounded. That was the worst that Carla could have heard. It was her biggest fear.

The only thing Carla didn't tell Portia about was her brother Pierson. She couldn't take the chance that Monster would find out about him, even accidentally. The fact that Payne was being seduced into the lifestyle his father lived was reason enough to keep that under her hat. Carla hoped that she could tell Portia and Payne about their younger brother one day soon.

Thinking of Pierson, Carla was reminded that she needed to talk with Terry about the changes to their weekend. She walked back into the building, wiping the water from her cheeks.

"Are you okay, boss lady," Maria asked, holding up a box of tissues.

Carla grabbed a couple of them and took a deep, steadying breath. She dabbed at her eyes. "I'm more than okay." She had never told any of her workers about her personal problems, but for some reason, words flew from her lips like bile coming from a hung-over person gripping the edge of a toilet. "That was my daughter. I haven't been that close to her since she was four years old. Her father and his mother have kept her and her brother from me."

"Ay Dios Mio," Maria said, shaking her head. "No wonder you are crying."

"Yeah, but I still have to be careful, and so does she. They won't be happy if they find out about this."

"What about your son?"

"I told her not to tell him about this yet."

The office phone rang, and as Maria answered it, Carla went to her office to call Terry about their weekend plans. She blew her nose and cleared her throat before sitting down with her phone as she entered her office.

She pulled up his number and pressed the send button. "Hi, sweetheart," he said when he answered.

"Hi. I have some bad news about this weekend."

"What's going on?"

"I have to cancel."

"Why? Is everything alright?"

Carla swallowed the lump in her throat. "There are some things that I haven't told you. My parents have custody of my son. They want to go away for the weekend, and Betty has invited us to visit her for the weekend."

There was a brief silence. *Say something, anything.* "What's his name?"

Okay, not what I was expecting. "Pierson. He's sixteen. I found out after I was sentenced that I was pregnant."

"Why do your parents still have custody?"

He doesn't sound outraged or anything. He's too calm about this. "I wanted him to be raised in a loving and disciplined household. Monster doesn't know about him, and I wanted to keep it that way."

Again, there was silence before Terry spoke. "Well, it seems that you are still coming to Dallas. I don't see why our plans have to change. You can still come and stay with me. I'd like to meet your son unless you don't want me to."

Carla sighed, smiling. *That could have gone much worse.* "Do you really want to meet him, or is this about Voodoo twat?"

Terry laughed before answering. "Of course, I want to meet him. I would also like some Voodoo magic cast on me."

Now she was laughing. "Okay. I'll take him out of school for the day. The drive is only about three hours. So, we can plan to have dinner together."

"Carla," Terry said, snickering. "You don't have to drive. I'm still sending the plane. We just won't be able to join the Mile High Club, that's all."

"I just assumed that –"

"That what, the plane is built for two? You know, I think we're going to have to talk about why you believe that people will always respond negatively. You set your expectations way too low."

"Yeah, but it keeps me from being disappointed all the time." She did keep the lowest expectations of people. Maybe he was right.

"Well, I can't speak for others, but I have no plans of disappointing you. I have to go to a meeting, but we can talk later tonight."

"Bye Terry."

**

Terry sat in his chair with his fingers intertwined, elbows resting on the thick leather armrests, staring into space. *Have I bitten off more than I can chew with Carla?* He was upset that she hadn't told him about her son. It made him wonder what else she may be keeping from him. Having secrets in a relationship wasn't a good thing. It was the reason his first marriage had failed. *That and Lindsey was a gold digger.* She kept secrets because she intended to live a lavish lifestyle off him, not with him. He closed his eyes. He didn't want to think that of Carla.

She had been through things that he would never understand, things he didn't know because they hadn't talked about it yet. *This is just the beginning of our relationship. We are still getting to know each other better. I care enough about her to see where this may lead.*

I just need to slow down a bit even though my heart and body are already in love with her. I need to keep my head and think of the future. What if my

114

instincts are wrong? What if she doesn't care for me the same way I care about her? What if she's using me? Did she come on to me so strongly as part of a plan or scheme? Did she pretend to be hard to get in the beginning just to reel me in? I wouldn't be the first man to fall for something like that, but I don't feel that about Carla. While she has secrets, she never outright lied to me.

Many questions were popping out in his mind like the elusive bigfoot creature. Showing himself for just a second and then retreating, making him wonder if what he thought he saw was real.

"Terry," Roman called from the doorway. "Are you ready for this meeting?"

Terry stood, putting on his jacket. "Yeah."

"I still can't believe that the men who tortured us in boarding school want to do a deal with us."

"Times change," Terry said, buttoning his jacket as he grabbed his things and followed Roman down the hall.

Chapter Twenty-Two

"What do you think of this one, Momma," Portia said, coming out of the dressing room.

A smile formed on Carla's face. She loved hearing her daughter say, Momma. She looked over the outfit Portia was wearing. "Everything looks good on you, but I think the color is wrong. Let's see if they have it in red."

She went back to the wrack of dresses and searched until she found what she wanted. She took it back to Portia's dressing room, "Here,"

"Thanks."

Carla went back to the chair she'd been sitting in. While Portia changed, Carla flipped through some reports she had stuck in her bag when she left the office. The numbers looked good to her. Carla had thoroughly read the statements the day before, but she wanted to give them one last look before calling her broker and telling him what her decision was.

"Yeah, I like this one better in red," her daughter said, looking at herself in the mirror.

"I agree," Carla told her. "Now, all you need are some shoes to go with it." It had only been a few days since their reunion, but it felt like they had been hanging out forever. She and Portia had talked on the phone, and when she asked Carla to help her pick out a dress for a first date with a nice young man she met a week before, Carla jumped at the chance to go.

"I saw some at a shop on the other end of the mall, which might be perfect," her child said as she went back to change into her clothes.

Carla continued looking over the report until Portia came out of the dressing room. Her phone rang, and she paused to take the ringing cell from her purse. "It's Grandma," she said, putting her finger to her lips to make sure Carla didn't say anything. "Hi, Gigi." Carla couldn't make out what was said on the other end of the phone. "I'm at the mall," Millie spoke. "I wanted a new dress for my date with Vaughn." More chatter came from Millie. Portia rolled her eyes and sighed as if she were over the conversation. "I can pick a dress without your help Grandma. I'm a grown woman." Millie's voice was louder, and she spoke quickly. "Bye Grandma."

"Is everything okay?" Carla asked, looking at the deflated look on her child's face.

"Everything's fine," she said with a grimace. "She just gets on my nerves sometimes."

"Trust me, I understand," Carla said, looping her arm into Portia's and moving her to the checkout. When the cashier told them the total of the dress, Carla handed the woman a couple hundred-dollar bills to cover the cost.

"I've got money," Portia said.

"I know, but this is the first thing I've been able to do for you in a long time."

"Thank you," Portia said, kissing her on the cheek.

"Let's go find those shoes," Carla said, grabbing the bag for her.

As they walked through the mall, Portia said, "I saw you reading something. It looked like work. You're not going to get in trouble for ditching work to shop with me, are you?"

"No," Carla grinned. *Should I tell her the truth?* "I can't get into trouble."

"Why not? Is your boss chill like that?"

"I am the boss," Carla said, watching her face.

"Yeah, but what about the big boss. The head honcho?"

"That's me. I am the B.L.I.C."

"What's that?"

"The boss lady in charge." Portia smiled at her. "I bought the company a while ago, but no one knows."

"Why not?"

"Well, because I don't need to brag about what I have. I don't ever want people to treat me better than I deserve, just because I own a business or have more money than they do."

"Wow, you and daddy are so different. All he does is brag and show off."

"Maybe that's why I'm the opposite. I don't want what I have to outweigh who I am." Carla saw what having money did to Monster. She determined never to think she was better or more deserving than someone else because of the size of her bank account or her possessions.

Thanks to the friends she made on the inside, Carla was doing well financially. Not that anyone could tell by how she lived. She had a stock portfolio that would shock anyone who knew her. She had also been smart with how to grow her shipping business.

To most, it only appeared that she worked for 3P shipping, but she owned it and a few other small shipping companies around the country. Carla not only got her G.E.D. in prison, but she also became a student of the people she was locked up with. She learned about finance, business, marketing, and a lot more. One lady showed her how to make pralines in a microwave. She picked up many new skills. She learned that people loved to talk about what they knew, and she listened carefully, keeping as much of that knowledge in her head until she was released.

After she and Portia found the shoes she wanted, they got something to eat in the food court. When they sat down, Portia asked, "Do you have any brothers and sisters? Are your mother and father still alive? I asked grandma and daddy, but they would only say I didn't need to know."

"My mom and dad are still alive, and I have a sister." Carla knew it was natural for Portia to be curious, and she wanted to tell her everything, but Carla held some of the truth back still. She did it for Pierson. "Eden, my sister lives in Dallas now. Your grandfather and grandmother are here in Houston, and someday soon, I hope you all will meet. They don't know about you and your brother. I kept it from them because I didn't think they loved me back when you were little. I never told them about you two because we still haven't healed all our wounds and forgiven each other." She could see the look of rejection on her daughter's face, and it broke her heart. "I'm sure that they will welcome you with open arms once they learn about you."

"Tell me about them. Anything, I just want to know something."

"Okay. Your grandmother loves the holidays, and I mean all of them. She spends weeks decorating for Halloween and Christmas. My dad he's kind and sweet. He's a minister."

"Really?"

Carla nodded. Carla told her about watching him prepare his sermons when she was a little girl. By the time they left the mall. She had told Portia so much that Carla felt sad for her kids missing out on knowing such great people.

Chapter Twenty-Three

Terry stood as his mother approached him. "Mother, you look lovelier than ever."

"Thank you," she said, sitting in the chair as he pulled it out for her. They studied their menus and gave their order to the waiter when he came. When they were alone, his mother asked, "How is business?"

"Do you remember the name, Malcolm Wainwright?"

"Of course, I do. He was that snobby little brat that gave you a hard time at boarding school. Him and Jeremy something or other, and the other little pig-faced boy."

"Jeremy Donaldson and Gregory Carmichael," Terry filled in for her. "Well, the three of them went into business together. Now it is failing. Someone is attempting a takeover, buying up stock from their shareholders. There is a lone hold-out. A man who wants more money. They came to Roman and me, hoping that we would loan them the money they need to save their company."

"Why would they come to you after all the things they put you and Roman through."

"That's precisely what Roman and I wanted to know. According to them, they never meant any real harm. They were just boys being boys. They figured that because Roman and I desperately wanted to be a part of their group back then, We might be willing to bury the hatchet and be friends now."

"What did you tell them?"

"I smiled and told them that all I ever wanted from them was to see Roman and me as equals. To get to know us on our character and not be so influenced by what we had or didn't have. Then I told them that while they only came to me because I have money, I would provide what was fair based on the content of their character, which was absolutely nothing because they had not changed in all the years since we were in school."

His mother smiled at him. "Good, because if you were going to sit here and tell me that you helped those little bastards, I would kick you in the worst place imaginable."

Terry laughed and took her hand, kissing it. "I love you, mother."

"I love you too. Now let's talk about when you can meet Ms. Snowden's daughter.

"Mom," Terry said, looking her in the eye. "I can't meet her. I'm involved in a relationship with someone."

"Who?"

"I can't tell you just yet. We haven't really discussed letting the world know we are involved." Though that wouldn't last long. *Since we are all attending the barbeque and likely to arrive together, you'll find out then.*

"I am not the world. I am your mother."

"I know, but until she and I have discussed this, I'm keeping it to myself."

"Fine," she said with a huff. "Are you planning to go to the barbeque at Betty's on Saturday?"

"Yes," he said, pausing as their food was placed before them. "I spoke to Billy about it this morning."

Chapter Twenty-Four

"Pierson, your mother's here, get your stuff," her mother yelled as she opened the door for Carla on Friday morning. "Don't forget your book bag," she added. "Hey, sugar," she said when Carla stepped into the entryway. They exchanged an awkward hug. "He has homework for his economics and history classes, due on Monday."

"Okay."

"Where are you guys staying. I talked to Betty yesterday, and she said that she hadn't heard back from you about attending."

I guess now is as good a time as any to throw out there that I have a boyfriend. It's not like the whole family won't know who it is by the end of the weekend. "We'll be staying with my gentleman friend. I forgot to tell Betty about it. I'll call her on the way to the airport."

Pierson came towards them with a duffle bag and a backpack. "Hi," he said, glancing quickly to Carla before dropping the duffle to hug his grandmother.

"You behave yourself and have a good time."

"I will," he responded when she let him go. He picked up his bag and slid past Carla, going out the door to the car.

"I gave him some spending money," her mother said, watching Pierson.

"You didn't have to do that."

"It's from the money you deposit into the account for him."

"Well, we'd better go. Tell dad, hello for me."

"Talk to him," she said, pointing to the car. "Give him some time. He loves you. He's just afraid to show it."

Carla nodded her head. *I know how he feels.* Carla gave her mother another hug and went to the car. Pierson played a game on his phone, and he was quiet most of the ride. Carla didn't know what to say to him. Then she got an idea. "What game are you playing?"

"Fortnite-Save the World."

"Oh, sounds interesting," Pierson said nothing else. *Well, that was a bust.*

He groaned and then put the phone away. Looking out the window. "Where are we? This is the wrong direction to get to Dallas."

"We're not driving. We're taking a private jet," Carla told him as she got off the highway.

Pierson turned to look at her. "You have a private jet?"

Carla shook her head. "No. The man that I'm dating does."

"Is he a drug dealer?"

Wow. I can't believe he just asked me that. Carla licked her lips. "No. He's a businessman."

"Who has his own jet? You're a liar."

Carla could hear the disdain and sarcasm dripping from his voice. "Pierson, I know that you don't like me or the fact that I'm your mother. I may not have been around for you the way I should have been, but regardless. You will speak to me with respect."

"Why should I? I don't know you. Grandma and Poppy raised me, not you. I didn't even want to come on this stupid trip."

Carla turned the car into the gas station and turned off the engine. She got out and walked around to his door, opening it. "Get out."

He looked at her as if she were crazy for a second. There was fear and defiance in his eyes. He took off his seatbelt and got out of the car. She slammed his door. "What? You gonna leave me here?"

"No, but I want to make damn sure you can see into my eyes while I'm talking. I want to make sure you understand what I'm about to say to you because I don't and won't repeat myself." She gestured to his ballcap, clothes, and the phone in his pocket. "Everything you have is because of me. Even the fucking air you breathe is because I gave you that. No, I didn't raise you because I was locked up for making dumb choices. You are blessed because I wanted you to have a better life. You should thank me for all that I have given up for you to be raised in a loving home. Do I wish I could have been there to see your first steps, hear your first word, and walk you to school? Absolutely I do, but I couldn't, so I made sure that you had the only other people on the planet who would love you the same way that I would. I've made sure that you have everything you've ever needed every day since I got home. All your clothes, games, and everything you have came from me. So, when you speak to me, you better remember that because what was given can be taken away. Now, you get your punk ass back in that car and watch how you talk to me from now on. If you can't be respectful, then be quiet."

Pierson got back in the car. Carla turned her back to him, closing her eyes. *I'm not going to cry. I'm not. Spoiled little shit. I know my mother and father taught him better than that.* After a few deep breaths, she returned to the car.

Chapter Twenty-Five

Terry was sitting in the back of the plane looking over some documents when Carla boarded. He got up, kissing her. "Hi," she said when he let her go. She looked off, upset. "Terry, this is my son Pierson."

He extended his hand to her son. "It's a pleasure to meet you, Pierson. Make yourself comfortable."

"Thanks," the young man said, moving to a seat near the front.

"We'll be ready to take off in a little while," his pilot told them.

"Come sit with me," Terry said, taking her hand. He tucked her into his side once they sat down. "What's wrong?"

"I don't want to talk about it."

"Alright," Terry said, caressing her shoulder as she lay her head on his. He could feel the tension between Pierson and his mother. Terry only had a basic understanding of their relationship from Carla's side of things. Maybe he would get a chance to talk to Pierson alone over the weekend.

Halfway through the flight, Carla fell asleep. He eased away from her, going to the front to speak with Pierson. "Hey," he said, sitting across from him. "Can we talk for a bit?"

Pierson removed his earbuds. "What's up?"

"Why was she upset when you guys got on the plane?"

He sighed, slumping in his seat. "I pissed her off in the car. I asked her if you were a drug dealer, and she lost it."

"A drug dealer? Why would you ask her that?"

Pierson waved his hand around. "Private jet. She used to be a drug dealer, and I knew she couldn't afford to have something like this. I didn't think she was dating a rich white man."

"So, you were rude to her, and you hurt her feelings because you made an assumption of who she is and who I am?"

"Yeah, I guess I was."

Terry watched as the fullness of what he'd done hit Pierson. "I'm going to be honest with you. You have no right to sit in judgment of her and what she may have done in the past. Before you assume something about her or anyone else, take the time to get to know them. Ask her about her past and how she ended up living the way she did."

"How did you meet her?"

"We met at a party. I thought she was incredibly beautiful, and I wanted to know her better. It took me a while to convince her to give me a shot. She's one tough cookie."

"Tell me about it. I never know what to say to her. I – just feel like she doesn't really care about me."

"That's why you need to talk to her. Ask her questions, but you also have to be open to hearing what she has to say. Maybe you can try that this weekend."

"Yeah, maybe," Pierson said, sighing.

Terry was sure that he was at a point where he should stop talking, or Pierson would tune him out. "Alright, I'm here too if you want to talk." He went back to his seat beside Carla. He had reports and other things he could work on." *It's not really my place to get in their issues, and I hope that Carla isn't upset when she finds out that I said something to her son.*

**

When they exited the plane, Carla and Terry rode in the back of the car. Pierson chose to ride in the front with the driver. "You don't do anything like normal people, do you?" She asked Terry as they rolled out of the private airport. "Do you actually have a regular car that you drive?"

Terry smiled. "I have several."

Carla shook her head. "Let me guess, they are all super expensive."

"What's the point of having money if you don't spend and enjoy it."

"I agree. Do you have a pool?" Pierson asked.

"Yes."

"Cool. Mom, do you know how to swim?"

He called me mom. Carla couldn't believe it. "Uh- yeah. Your grandpa taught me and Cousin Betty when we were little."

"He taught me too."

Carla looked at Terry with wonder. He humped his shoulders, making a face. *I know you had something to do with this change.* She smiled as he squeezed her hand. She mouthed the words, "Thank you." He kissed her hand.

**

"Are you going to tell me what you said to him?" Carla asked Terry as they lay in bed together.

"No," he said, kissing the top of her head. "We talked, and that's all you need to know."

Carla shifted from his side to lay on top of Terry, who lay with his hands under his head. She kissed his chin. "Fine. If you won't tell me about your conversation, we need to find something else to do 'cause I'm not sleepy yet."

"How about a bath?"

"Oooh, yes."

They got up and went into the bathroom together. When he gave her the tour of his mansion, she fell in love with the bathtub. It was big enough for several people. Carla stood back and watched Terry turned on the water and then walked around the bathroom naked. *He's got a great ass for a white man. I bet there's a black man in his family tree. Where else could the Watson boys get them big dicks from?*

"What?" Terry said when he looked in the mirror and caught her staring at him.

"Nothing. I'm just admiring the view."

He turned. "Which would you prefer, lavender or rose petals? I ordered them for you when you agreed to come for the weekend."

Carla looked at the bath bombs. "Let's try the rose one."

Terry turned off the tap when the tub was full, and Carla dropped the ball in. It fizzed and bubbled as it dissolved into the water, filling the bathroom with the scent of roses. "Mmm, I like that," she said, inhaling deeply.

Carla dug into her toiletry bag and found a hair clip, putting her hair up. Terry gathered some fluffy white towels, setting them beside the tub. He held Carla's hand as she stepped into it. Then he got in behind her.

They relaxed, and Terry began to massage her shoulders. "That feels good," Carla said, letting her head fall forward.

"What do you think our family will think of us dating?"

"I think they'll be surprised, but ultimately it doesn't matter. It only matters what we think, right?"

"Right," Terry answered, rubbing circles on her back. "Are you nervous about meeting my mother?"

Carla shook her head. "Should I be?"

"No, but I should warn you that she'll want to know everything about you. I told you she's been determined to find me a wife."

"Do you want a wife?"

"Someday. How about you? If you get divorced from Monster, do you think you'll get married again?"

"I don't ever want to be married again."

"Ever?"

Carla closed her eyes and took a deep breath. "Ever." She turned so that she faced him. "You have to understand it from my point of view. Marriage is like slavery, bondage. I don't ever want to be enslaved to another person as long as I live."

"Not every marriage is a bad experience. I had trouble too, but I still believe in it."

"It's not the same. Your spouse didn't control every facet of your life. You chose your wife. You loved her. I didn't choose Monster, and I damn sure didn't love that son of a bitch." Carla's anger snuck up on her. She wasn't expecting to talk about this. She got up and grabbed a towel, getting out. "I was held captive and abused by the man who held the title of husband. That's why I don't want another one."

Chapter Twenty-Six

As Terry got out of the tub, Carla left the bathroom. She had put on a bathrobe and was standing on the balcony overlooking the gardens when he got into the bedroom. Terry dropped his towel and put on a robe as well. He joined her, wrapping his arms around her. "I'm sorry sweetheart. I didn't mean to upset you." He could feel her body expand, and she took a deep breath.

She turned to look at him. "We need to get something straight right now. If you are a man that has to put a ring on it and have a piece of paper saying that we belong to each other, we need to end it now. I'm never going to be that woman."

"I could understand you better if you told me what you've been through with this guy. I want to understand what you experienced and why you feel this way."

Carla pulled away from him. "Do you really want to know?"

"Yes. Tell me everything."

"Sit down." Terry sat down on the settee.

**

After telling him everything, he may just tell me to leave and never return. Carla leaned against the balcony railing. "Once upon a time, I was a good girl, a good student. I embodied what my mother and father preached. I was twelve when Eden was born, and my parents weren't focused on me for the first time in my life. Maybe I was a bit jealous of my new little sister. I can't honestly say that, but a new family moved in up the block from us." Carla turned and joined Terry. "The girl was my age, and she caught up to me one day walking home, and we started talking. She seemed nice, but she had a rebellious streak a mile wide. At first, I tried not to get caught up in what she did, but we became friends. We hung out at school, and we walked home together. Then one day, I decided that it wouldn't hurt to try a few new things, like pot. I smoked with her. Betty and I hung out a lot until then, but I started ditching her to hang out with Nelda." Carla crossed her legs. "I started skipping school, and that's when my mother and father found out that I was misbehaving. They sat me down and talked to me about my choices."

"Did they know you were smoking weed?"

Carla's eyebrows raised as she shook her head. "No. Thanks to everything Nelda taught me, I got really good at hiding it. By the time I was nearly sixteen, I had graduated from weed to coke. Nelda always found a way to get it. I had no idea what it cost or where it came from. I didn't care. I liked getting high. I felt powerful." Carla looked off into the distance. She was too afraid to look at Terry. "Once when Nelda's parents were out of town, she threw a party, and that's where I met Ronnie. He was cute and a few years older. I could blame it on being high, but I let him take my virginity that night. I barely remembered it the next day, but he showed up at Nelda's a few days later with something new for us to try." She took a deep breath. "He told us it was better than anything we had ever tried, and it was."

"What was it?"

**

Terry couldn't believe it when she said, "Crack cocaine. One hit and we were addicted. That's when my life really went to hell. I chased that high hoping to feel like I did that first time. It got so bad that I would steal – she closed her eyes. "- I robbed people, broke into houses and business and take all kinds of things to get more." Terry reached for her hand. Carla shook it off and got up, moving away from him.

"What happened then?" Terry asked.

She took a long breath. "Nelda and I would run into each other occasionally, but we were running in different circles. She had started using heroine. I wasn't willing to inject anything into my body. Then I found out that she had overdosed. I had been in a tug of war with my parents. They would come find me and bring me home, preaching and talking to me about my choices. The minute they left me alone for a second, I stole from them and took off, always running back to Ronnie. The drugs were more important. After Nelda died, my parents found me and gave me an ultimatum. I could get clean, and they would help, or I could leave and never come back. I left. That's when I met Will."

"Monster, how?"

Carla nodded and blew air out of her mouth. "Ronnie took me to meet him. I didn't know that Ronnie was trading me to him to save his own life. He'd stolen drugs and money from Monster. Monster told him that he'd wipe his debt clean if he brought me to him. He moved me into his house and refused to let me have any drugs. I was forced to quit cold turkey. That's the only thing he did for me that would be considered good. Once I was clean Monster kept tabs on me. I wasn't allowed to leave his house without him or Hammer. He took care of me. He was nice. He talked to me sweetly and I had everything I could ever want. At first, I felt lucky. Then one day he slipped into my room. I could tell he was drunk probably high. He told me it was time to pay up and he started taking off his clothes. I told him no, that I didn't want to fuck him. I told him I would pay him back for all he'd done. That's when I got to know the real Monster. I could say that it wasn't rape – because I just gave in when I realized that it would be easier than fighting him. After that, he bragged about finally having me. He told everyone that I was his girl and that he'd kill anyone who touched me. He was jealous of anyone and everyone. He would accuse me of flirting with Hammer and anyone else that looked at me twice. It was a long time before I found out why he seemed obsessed with me. Apparently, he'd tried to flirt with me at a club or something. I don't even remember meeting him. I rejected him and that was something that no one ever did. He was determined to have me after that. So, when he found out that Ronnie and I were associated, he used it to get me. I put up with his shit because I didn't have anywhere else to go. My family didn't want me around. I was an embarrassment to my father and mother. My cousin Betty had been my only friend besides Nelda, and Betty had the good sense to distance herself from me when I lost my mind. I didn't have a job. I hadn't finished school. The only thing I knew how to do was fuck and get high."

"So, you stayed with Monster, for how long?"

Carla finally looked at Terry. "I stayed with him twenty-one years. I might still be with him if I hadn't gone to prison."

"And you never tried to leave him?" Terry asked curiously.

"I tried a few times, but the punishments for leaving got so bad that I lost hope and believed it was my penance for all the horrible things I did. I thought God was punishing me for being a horrible person."

"Men who hit women are repulsive and the fact that he forced himself on you makes me want to kill him."

"I've had more broken bones and concussions than you can imagine. I had a hard time learning not to say what popped into my head, especially where he was concerned. Not that it took me saying anything, for him to hit me." Terry knew that color was flooding his face. His lips were a thin line. A man putting his hands on a woman was reprehensible. "I hate to admit it, but I got pregnant hoping that it would keep him from hitting me. It worked for a while. When I got pregnant the first time, I knew I had to find a way out. I didn't want my child raised in that environment. I had to be smart about it, but how? I had to wait and watch for some way to get money and stash it. Then one day Monster got popped for a small transaction and I was there. The police did everything they could to get me to tell them what I knew. That's when I realized that I held more power than I thought. I knew everything about his dealings. He talked freely around me because he never considered me a threat. He may not have been the sharpest tool in the shed, but he was smart enough to marry me. I was his wife for the simple fact that I couldn't be forced to testify against him. After a while, I wasn't under constant watch and sometimes he sent me to do drug drops and money collections. That's when I started stealing his money. He was slipping and wasn't checking the cash counts because he trusted me. So, I stole from him and stashed money somewhere he would never think to look for it. Just when I thought I had enough money to leave him and Houston behind for good, I got pinched with his drugs and money. Again, the feds wanted me to turn on him, but I wouldn't."

"Why not. That could have been your way out?"

"Fear. I was too afraid of what he might do to me. Besides he had my children. I did ten years in prison while his mother raised my kids, teaching them to hate me. After I got out, I refused to go back to him. So, he has refused to let me see my children unless I went home where I belonged as he says. I have stayed away from them and him because I have a bigger secret."

"What?"

"I was pregnant when I was arrested. I didn't find out until my plea deal was accepted. I never told Monster. For the first time since my parents cast me out, I called them. I didn't tell them all that I went through, but I asked them to take my baby into their home when he was born. I never told Monster who my family was. My folks don't know anything about Monster. I figured it was the only way to keep Pierson from falling under his control. If I could have gotten Portia and Payne away from him, I would have. So, I have three children. Portia came to me last week. I'm afraid of what will happen if her grandmother and father find out. I want to tell her about Pierson, but I can't take the chance of them finding out about him.

"I assume that Pierson doesn't carry his father's last name."

"No, I didn't name him Johnson. I gave him my maiden name, Baxter."

"You've been keeping secrets from everyone in your life."

"Yes, and I have to keep it that way."

"Come here," Terry said, holding out his hand to her. When she took it, he pulled her into his lap. "I don't blame you for feeling the way you do. I'm sorry for everything that you have been through. I would never force you to do anything you don't want to." *Tell her how you feel.* "You are an amazing woman. I promise you that I won't ever bring up the subject of marriage again. Just know that if you change your mind, you'll have to propose to me, deal?"

Carla giggled. "Deal," Carla agreed before she kissed him.

Chapter Twenty-Seven

Carla was alone when she woke the next morning. After getting dressed, she walked through Terry's house trying to find the kitchen. *This house is way too big. All I want is a cup of coffee. There's no reason this single man should be living in such an enormous house.* "Excuse me," she said to the man Terry introduced as his houseman. "I can't find the kitchen."

He smiled and nodded. "This way Madam."

Carla shook her head as she followed the man down the hall. At the end of it he pushed open a swinging door. Carla stepped inside to find Pierson and Terry at the stove.

"Morning," she said when they turned to look at her. "Thank you," she added to Terry's houseman.

"Morning Sweetheart," Terry said coming around to kiss her. "We're making breakfast. Sit down."

"I need coffee," Carla told him as she sat on a stool at the counter. "I'm surprised you don't have a chef or something."

Terry placed a mug of coffee and a beautiful decanter of cream in front of her. "I do, but I gave her the day off. Would you like sugar?"

"No," Carla shook her head.

"Guess what I learned?" Terry asked turning back to watch Pierson. "Your son is an artist. Here he said, picking up a plate and sitting it down near her mug.

Carla looked at the pancake on the plate. It looked like Terry. "Wow. That's awesome."

"Come look at how he does it," Terry said taking her hand.

Carla got up and moved around the counter, standing near Pierson. "It's not that hard to do. You just cook some parts a little longer that others," he told her as he used a bottle with a pointed tip to put batter in the pan.

"I couldn't do that," Carla said watching him. When he was finished with squirting mix into specific places, he waited a second or two. Then he flipped it over.

Carla gasped. "That's me."

"Yup," Pierson said beaming with pride. He put the pancake on a plate and handed it to her.

"Are you going to make one with your face?" Carla handed the plate in her hand to Terry.

"Nah, I got something better in mind."

Carla stood watching as he repeated his process. He flipped it over, and Carla gasped again. "That's Cardi B."

Pierson put the last pancake on a plate and sat it on the island counter with the other. "Which one do you want?" He asked Carla.

"I'll take Cardi B. I couldn't eat myself."

"I'll eat your mom," Terry said. They all froze and started laughing at the same time.

"That's something I don't ever want to hear again," Pierson said shaking his head.

"How did you learn to do this?"

"I watched a guy on a video do it. It looked easy and I like to draw. It's not hard but it took be a while to get it right."

Did I get off that plane in the twilight zone? My son called me mom, and he's laughing with me as if we've never had any problems. I should be thanking God, but I can't help but wonder what the hell is happening.

**

After breakfast, Terry went to his study to do some work. Pierson was enjoying himself in the pool. Carla sat on the balcony with her phone. She realized that she hadn't called Betty as she said she would. She dialed her number and waited. "Hey Carla," Betty said when she answered the phone.

"Hey Betty Boop. I'm sorry I didn't call you yesterday to tell you that I wasn't going to be staying with you."

"Don't worry. I already heard through the momma grapevine. As soon as you left your mother's house, she called my momma, who then called me. So, you've got a boyfriend in Dallas. Tell me about him."

Carla should have known her mother was spilling tea all over the place. "No. You can just wait until this afternoon."

"You're bringing him with you?"

"Yes."

"Okay, but you have to give me something."

"Well, I can tell you that he's just what I need in my life."

"That's all you're going to give me?"

"Yup. We'll see you in a few hours. Bye," Carla smiled as she swiped the red button on her screen.

Terry had broken through her glass cage she had built around herself. Carla had no idea when she saw him for the first time that he would be the one to make her see that she could share herself with someone and not get hurt at every turn.

He not only gave her what she wanted which was physical pleasure, he gave her intimacy, and acceptance which was the most important of all. Terry also gave her something she didn't think she might ever have. She and her son were communicating without animosity for the first time in his life. *He gave me a connection to Pierson. I love him for that. I love him. Nooooo.* Carla's heart raced, beating frantically in her chest. *I can't love him. Then why does my heart feel like it weighs a ton? It's because he's filling it up. You love him, admit it.* "Fuck me sideways," Carla said softly.

"We can try that, but you'll have to show me that position," Terry said coming up behind her.

Carla swung around, surprised that he was there. The full force of her feeling filled her like hot air in a balloon. She felt like she was going to float away. *What do I do now?*

Chapter Twenty-Eight

The look on Tanya's face as she opened the door to Carla, Terry, and Pierson when they arrived was priceless. Her mouth hung open and her eyes grew ten times their normal size. "Come in, come in," she finally said. She hugged Pierson first. "Everyone is in the back yard," she told Pierson as she pointed towards the kitchen when she let him go to hug her brother-in-law. "I thought you just wanted to get the D," she whispered in Carla's ear when she hugged her.

Carla waited until she was sure Terry and Pierson couldn't hear. "I did, but he had other plans. I should have listened to you when you said it would be hard to walk away from the magic stick."

They both giggled. "Come on, you can help me and Betty in the kitchen." She followed her cousin through the house.

"What you mean to say is that you and Betty Boop want to get in my business and get the dirty details."

"It's not like you're gonna tell us anything. You never do."

Carla didn't let the dig at her need for privacy bother her. Since she had opened up to Terry, she knew that she would have to come clean with everyone about some of her secrets, but she would not talk about her sex life with her cousins.

Betty was elbow deep in potato salad when they walked into the kitchen. She stopped and looked through the glass door to the back yard. "So, Terry is your new boo thang?"

Tanya moved around the counter and got to work cutting fruit for a tray. Carla planted her hand on the counter. "Yes. We've been seeing each other since the engagement party." Betty shook her head and got back to making her dish. "What?"

"I want to know how it happened, but you tend to keep everything to yourself."

"At first, it was just going to be about sex, but he found out where I worked and showed up at my job. I was still trying to keep it from being more than physical, but he said he wanted more. He convinced me to give it a shot."

Tanya snickered, "He used his magic stick to cast a spell on her."

"Shut up, T.T." Carla rolled her eyes playfully.

"So does it run in the family?" Tanya asked, looking over her shoulder at Carla. Carla closed her eyes and pressed her lips together. "It does," Tanya said looking at Betty. "I can't wait to talk to Eden when she gets back from camping."

"Camping?" Carla didn't believe what she had just heard.

"Yup," Tanya said grinning. Carl, the biker took her camping this week before she starts her new job."

"A get-away for two," Betty added.

"Hey, what are the odds that the four of us would fall for white men in the same family?"

"Did you just say fall for. Does that mean that you are in love with Terry?" Tanya said, putting down her knife.

Carla closed her eyes and gritted her teeth. *Damn it! I didn't mean to say that.* "No. You know what I mean."

"Don't lie to us." Betty accused, putting the potato salad into a long pan.

The back door opened. "Sweetie, come outside. I want to introduce you to my mother," Terry said.

Betty and Tanya stared at her, grinning from ear to ear. *I should have kept my mouth shut. They are going to mess with me for the rest of the day.*

Carla remembered seeing Mrs. Watson at the party, but she looked different in casual clothes. She was still elegant and classy, but she didn't seem as intimidating in slacks and a bright yellow blouse. "Mom this is my girlfriend, Carla."

Carla took a seat beside Mrs. Watson on the swinging loveseat. Terry's mother shooed him away. "Go away and let me talk to the woman who has put an end to my matchmaking efforts." Carla winked at Terry as he left them. His mother turned to face Carla. "Well, you're a looker for sure. Though I'd expect nothing less for Terry."

"Thank you."

"I spoke to your son for a bit. He's well-mannered and polite."

"The credit for that goes to my parents. They have raised him." Carla waited for her to ask why. She didn't.

"Carla, I'll be Eighty on my next birthday in August. I figure that each day that I wake up and make it through is a blessing. I could get the call from God to join my husband in heaven at any time. So, I'm going to cut straight to it. Terry's ex-wife Lindsey was a money-grubbing gold digger who broke his heart. Who are you and what do you want from my son?"

Carla took a deep breath, putting her hand on Mrs. Watson's. She looked into the eyes the same color as Terry's. "Mrs. Watson, I like your bluntness. I'm going to be just as forthcoming with you. I was after one thing when I met him, and it wasn't his money." She looked at Terry. "We've only known each other for two weeks, but now, I want everything he has, and I don't mean his money, house, or anything financial. I haven't told Terry this yet, but I'm well off. I own the company that he thinks I work for, and I'm constantly building and growing that business to pass it down to my children. I come with a lot of baggage and so far, Terry has shown me that he can accept it and is willing to help me carry it. I care a great deal for him, and I promise that I have no intentions of hurting him."

**

Terry tried not to stare, but it seemed as if his mother and Carla were having a very serious conversation. "Their holding hands," Mike said handing Terry a drink.

"That's got to be good," Billy added as he worked the grill.

"I hope so," Terry said, taking a drink from the bottle in his hand. "Carla means a great deal to me."

"Does that mean what it sounds like?" Billy asked. "Are we going to be adding a sister to our quickly expanding family?"

Terry shook his head. "No."

"Wait, what?" Mike looked confused.

"My sweetie doesn't want to get married ever."

"All women want to get married," his brothers said in unison.

"Not that one," Terry said taking another drink. "It's okay though. I'll be content to be with her. A piece of paper and a ring isn't important." *My love for her is all that matters.*

He looked across the yard to where they had been sitting. His mother was coming towards him. Carla was going back inside. His mother kissed his cheek. "I like her a lot. I'm going to see if me and Ella can get Pierson to show us how to Tik Tok. I hear it's the big new thing."

Terry and his brother's watched their mother walk away before they all burst into laughter. "Our mother wants to learn how to Tik Tok," Mike said howling.

Chapter Twenty-Nine

Being in love sucks ass. I don't want to leave him. Carla held on to Terry, breathing in his cologne. *I never did give him his shirt back or tell him about his cufflink.* She pulled away from him. "I don't want to go."

"Then don't," Terry said, sounding just as melancholy as Carla.

"Pierson has school tomorrow."

"We'll enroll him in a school here."

Carla smiled and then giggled. "You're not making this easier."

"Sorry," Terry said, kissing her again. "Go," he said stepping back from the stairs to the plane.

They had decided that Terry wouldn't fly to Houston with them. They both thought that it would make things easier. *We were wrong about that.* Carla climbed the stairs, looking back and waving goodbye.

She took a seat close to Pierson, but where she could see Terry as he stood watching the door close. Then he got in his car as the plane's engines fired up.

She blew him a kiss as he looked back at the plane one last time.

Once they were in the air, Pierson said, "While you were saying goodbye to Terry, Grandma called. They're staying one more night and coming home tomorrow. She wants me to stay with you tonight."

"Okay. Do you need to go home for anything?"

"No. I have something I can wear to school and the rest of my books are in my locker."

"Sounds like we're all good then."

Pierson nodded and put his headphones back on.

Carla looked out the window, thinking about how strange life could be. A few weeks ago, she was sneaking into the gym to watch him play. Now, he was spending the night at her house. Carla had a burgeoning relationship with two of her three kids.

**

"Can I ask you something?" Pierson asked, sitting down at the kitchen table.

Carla was busy making sauce for their spaghetti dinner. "Ask away," Carla told him adding seasoning to the sauce.

"Where's my father?"

Carla wasn't expecting that. "You don't need to know that. He is not a good man. He's still living the life of a thug and criminal."

"He's in Houston, isn't he?"

"Why do you want to know? If you have some fantasy version of what it would be like to meet him someday, forget it. He's not going to hug you and tell you how happy he is to finally know about you."

"How do you know that? Grandma and Grandpa say that they thought you would never turn your life around, but you did. Maybe he has too or maybe he will."

Just breathe. Carla lowered the fire under the sauce. She sat down by her son. "Pierson, listen to me. I have seen him recently and – he hasn't changed. He doesn't want to change. I don't want to tell you the details of his personality, and the torture I went through living with him but trust me when I say that you are better off not knowing him."

He looked at her closely. She felt as if he were examining her soul. "Okay. He obviously hurt you really bad. I'm sorry that I asked."

Carla stood, putting her hand on his shoulder. "It's okay. Dinner is almost ready, go wash your hands."

He did as she asked. There were many things that she wanted to tell him, but she felt that if she told him about his sister and brother, he might try to find them.

**

"I am not going to do that," Carla said to Terry. He called just as she got in bed. "My son is in the bedroom down the hall, and my house isn't as big as yours. That means that he could hear me."

"Chicken."

"Am not," Carla said turning out the light.

"I can't be there to make you cum myself, so you have to do it while I listen."

"No."

"Boc, boc," he made noises like a chicken.

"I can't believe you," Carla said as Terry laughed and made more chicken noises.

"I know you're not wearing panties. Touch your clit like it's me using my tongue against it."

I don't know why I'm doing this. Carla's hand slid beneath the covers. She licked her lips, closing her eyes. *I'm not doing this.* She moved her hand back outside the covers.

"Are you doing it?"

"Mm, hmm."

"Keep rubbing and tell me how wet you are."

Carla hissed. "I'm very wet," she whispered. "Are you jerking off?"

"Yes sweetheart. It feels good, but I wish I was inside you."

"I wish you were too," Carla said, covering the phone with her hand. *If you only knew that I'm faking it. Oh, you would be so mad.* She sobered for a moment. *What if he's faking it too? Nah, guys don't know anything about faking sex.* Carla continued to moan and make Terry think she was masturbating until he finished with a groan and heavy breathing.

"Sweetie, that was great. Did you finish?"

Carla had to stop laughing to answer him. She whispered breathlessly, "Yes."

"Good, now get some sleep and I'll call you tomorrow."

"Nigh-night." Carla plugged her phone into the charger and snuggled under the covers, still giggling. *Better to fake it over the phone than in person.*

Chapter Thirty

Terry paced back and forth in front of the window in his office. "Tell me what's on your mind," Roman said, watching his friend wear down a strip of the carpet.

"I've been thinking about the deal Malcom pitched to us. I can't believe that we've never considered starting our own distribution division. We've thrown the thought out here and there, but never really discussed it. We wouldn't have to hire services to transport our goods to retail establishments if we had one. We could even distribute for our government contracts."

"So, are you saying you want to help Malcom Wainwright?"

"Oh, hell no," Terry said moving to sit in his chair. "I'm thinking of something altogether different." He tapped his fingers on his desk.

Roman looked at him for only a second. "The girlfriend? What are you considering, merging with a marriage?"

"No marriage, but a job offer that comes with great benefits. She can run the division. I'd just have to convince her to leave her current job and move to Dallas."

"What are we talking about, a title, generous salary, and mid-day quickies in the conference room with the boss?"

"Ha – ha, very funny, but yes."

Roman inhaled deeply. "I admit adding a distribution division is something we should have considered a while ago, but what if your relationship with her doesn't work out? Then you'll have an employee you've seen naked working closely with you every day."

"She's a professional. She wouldn't behave crazily, and I have no intention of us parting ways."

Roman nodded his head slowly. "Alright."

"I'll feel her out about it. In the meantime, look this over. It will give you an idea of what I have in mind," Terry told him, sliding a bound report across the desk."

"Okay. Are you ready for the trip to D.C.?"

"Nearly, we can get together later this afternoon and go over the contracts."

"I'll see you later then," Roman said leaving Terry's office.

**

By the time Carla came out of her bedroom, Pierson was dressed and in the kitchen. "Your coffee is ready. I heard you moving around so I made you a cup."

"Thank you," Carla said, sitting at the table. Pierson was washing a frying pan and a few other things. "What did you have for breakfast?"

"Eggs and toast." He put the last dish in the drain board and turned, leaning against the counter. "Mom, I had fun this weekend, and I'm sorry for what I said to you on Friday. I just wanted you to know that."

I really don't know what to think. We've had some kind of break through this weekend. "I'm glad. I enjoyed it too."

"Terry's a good guy. Do you think you will move to Dallas to be with him?"

Where on earth did that come from? "That's something that would be further down the road, I think. We haven't been dating long enough to think about things like that." She looked at the clock above the stove. "You should get your stuff so that we can get going."

All the way to his school, Carla wondered why he asked her about moving to Dallas. *Is he afraid that I'm going to disappear out of his life?* When she stopped near the entrance to the school, she said, "Pierson, I need you to know that spending this weekend with you means the world to me. I'm not planning to move away. I would like us to spend more time together. I love you. I always have." She leaned over hugging him. Then she kissed his cheek. "Have a good day."

He smiled at her. "Bye mom." He got out and just before he closed the door, he said, "I love you too."

Carla could barely see through the tears that blinded her as she maneuvered her car through the drop off lane. That feeling that her heart was full, hit her again, but exponentially. It couldn't be real. All that was happening to her seemed too good to be true. Carla pulled over as soon as she got to a side street leading to the main road. She wiped her eyes and more tears rained down.

When she finally got her emotions under control, she clasped her hands together, looking up. "Lord, I know this is you, but I couldn't stand it if something happens to shatter the happiness I feel right now. Thank you for whatever it is that you are doing up there. I know you have a plan for everything. Just don't let my happiness dam burst."

**

After lunch, Carla's cell phone rang, bringing her a flood. "Mom," Portia whispered, and Carla's heart dropped.

"What's wrong baby?"

"Gigi found out about me spending time with you. She's been tracking my phone."

I should have known. "Hey, don't worry about it. Everything's going to be alright."

"She called daddy and told him that he has to do something about you."

Something? Like what? Carla could hear Millie in the background, yelling her daughter's name.

"I have to go," Portia said then hung up.

Carla sat there for a minute. *They wouldn't hurt Portia for this, Would they? Nah.* There was another option on how to handle the situation. She could go see Millie. Maybe they could be adults about this.

Chapter Thirty-One

Carla knocked and took a step back while she waited. The door opened. "What the fuck are you doing on my doorstep?" Millie growled when she saw Carla. "I know yo trifling ass didn't come to my damn house."

"Millie, can we just talk like adults. I just want to talk to you. I didn't come here to start trouble."

"You ain't been nothing but trouble since the day you showed up at Will's house."

"I just want to make sure that Portia's okay."

"Gigi, please," Portia begged from behind her.

Millie turned and pointed. "You take yo ass back to yo room, right now," she yelled. "You still live under my roof, and you gone do what I say do." She turned to face Carla, again. "She's fine. You saw her. Now get off my property before I start shooting."

"Millie –"

"I'm not playing with you," Millie said, moving her hand behind her back.

Carla backed away. *Better safe than sorry.* "It doesn't have to be like this." Millie said nothing.

Tires screeched behind her. Carla turned just as Monster got out of his car coming towards her. *I should have gone home and got the gun.*

He got right in her face. "What the fuck you doing here? I told you to stay away from them damn kids unless you ready to be a family again. "

"You can't keep them from seeing me if they want. They are both old enough to decide for themselves," Carla said, not backing down.

Monster's arm came up grabbing a fist full of Carla's hair. He started to drag her towards his car. "You listen to me bitch –"

Before he could do whatever he intended, Carla kneed him in the groin. He let her go as he doubled over, grabbing his dick and balls. She elbowed him in the back, making him fall to the ground. Then she kicked him in the head. "If you ever put your hands on me again, I'll fuckin kill you Monster!"

Carla looked back to see Millie just as she heard sirens in the background. Portia was in the bedroom window crying. *This is not what I wanted.* She didn't want to deal with the police. She got in her car and left, but not before backing into that orange monstrosity that Monster loved to drive around. She didn't care that she dented the tail end of her Honda CR-V. It was worth it to see the front of his car totally fucked.

**

Carla didn't go back to work. She was amped up. She went home instead. When she got out of her car, Carla examined the damage to the back. *It's not as bad as it could be. The taillights are still intact.*

She'd see about putting it in the shop later. *I need a drink.*

She tried to call Portia but got the message that the caller was unavailable. *Millie must have taken her phone and blocked my number. At least, I know she's unharmed.* Carla poured herself a drink and stood at the counter. She wished she could see Monster's face when he saw the car. He'd been shocked enough that she fought back. It was the first time she'd ever defended herself from him physically.

Carla was just starting to feel calm when her phone rang. She checked the caller I.D. She took a deep breath before swiping the green button. "Hey there."

"Hi sweetheart," Terry said. "How's your day going so far?"

Don't tell him. He doesn't need to know. She must have taken too long to answer.

"What's wrong?"

Carla could hear the concern in his voice. "Nothing really. Millie found out that Portia has been seeing me and flipped out. I think she took her phone and blocked my number." *Don't tell him the rest. He doesn't need to know about my confrontation with Monster.*

"Sweetie, I'm sorry. What can I do to help?"

That right there, is enough. She sighed. "Nothing, except what you are doing. It means a lot that you care enough to ask."

"Of course I care."

"I'll figure it out." She wanted to change the subject. "How is your day going?"

"Pretty good. My partner and I have been talking about a way to grow our business and we came up with a great idea."

"What is it?"

"I'll tell you about it next week. I wanted to come to Houston this weekend, but I've got a business trip to D.C. later in the week and I'm supposed to be there through Monday. I wish you could come with me. We could do that mile-high thing."

Carla laughed. "That would be fun, but I can't take off for that long."

"I knew you were going to say that."

"I may be able to sneak away for a day trip to Dallas next week, but you would have to take the day off to spend with me."

"I think I could arrange that. My assistant is signaling me for a call. I miss you like crazy, and I'll call you soon."

"Bye Terry," Carla said kissing him through the phone.

Chapter Thirty-Two

The rest of Monday went along with no issues. Monster never showed up at her house. She didn't get any phone calls regarding his car. So, he must not have contacted his insurance company or the police. It shouldn't have surprised her though. There was no way in hell Monster would want to talk to the police. Not even to report her as a hit and run driver.

That would bring too much attention from the police into his life, and he couldn't have that. Monster could afford to get the car fixed or buy a new one without blinking an eye. *I have nothing to worry about from the police. I just have to watch my back.*

When her mother called later that evening, Carla was more relaxed, but still a bit on edge. "Hi momma."

"I should have called you as soon as we got back, but I wanted to get the house keeping out of the way. Then Pierson came in and talked my ear off about how much fun he had with you and Terry."

"We had fun with him too."

"I'm so glad to hear that. You know, with your father turning seventy-five we've been talking about him stepping down from the church so we can do some of the things old people should be doing, like traveling."

"That's awesome."

"I don't want to rush anything, but if you two started spending more time together, maybe by the time your father's ready to let go of the church Pierson could move in with you. What do you think of that?"

"We'll work our way up to that. I don't want to push Pierson to do anything he doesn't want to." *I'm still concerned about Monster finding out that Pierson is his, but I could always lie and say I slept with someone else if I need to.* She had nothing to worry about as long as they didn't do a DNA test.

Trying to handle her own divorce had been frustrating especially when Monster would sign the final papers. Being married at the time her son was born is what caused the legal issue of Monster having any parental rights. The law could side with him saying that she had no right to give guardian ship to her parents. Carla hoped never to be in a position that the judge would decide if Monster could have access to Pierson.

**

Tuesday Carla spent most of the day on the phone with her stockbroker, discussing her portfolio and some stock she was trying very hard to buy. "The final order of business for this call is the hold-out on the WDC stock. He's not going to sell unless we offer him more money."

"I need his shares. That's the only way my plans can move forward." She closed her eyes and leaned her head back against her chair. "Add three percent to the proposal, but this is our final offer. Make sure that he understands that if he says no, we are out."

"Okay."

"Owen, if the answer is no. Sell everything we've bought in WDC and let's start working towards Allied. It'll cost a lot more, but the end result will be the same. I'll have a bigger market share of the distribution industry."

"I'm on it," he said, disconnecting.

Carla wished she could pay Sandra back for teaching her about the stock market. Every bit of knowledge that woman had, she passed it on to Carla. It wasn't as simple as buying low and selling high.

Investing in the right companies at the right time is how people got wealthy. Rich was having a lot of money. Wealth was something that could be passed on for generations and it didn't diminish. It kept growing. That's what Carla was after. She knew that she could have it someday. She only needed the right distribution company to get her started. After that she would start looking at shipping around the world. For now, she only wanted to expand to ship across country and into Canada and Mexico.

When Carla got moved into the cell with Sandra, she had no idea that she was being placed with someone who would truly change her life. Most people avoided Sandra because she was a lifer. Those people convicted knowing that they had no chance of ever being set free could be unpredictable and dangerous.

Sandra had been convicted of murder. That's all anyone knew. That and she hadn't received the death penalty. The judge granted her mercy. That's how she ended up avoiding life on death row and execution.

It was Carla's bluntness that won Sandra over. The day she sat her things on the bunk above Sandra's, she introduced herself. "I'm Carla Baxter. If we're going to be living together for who knows how long, I want to know if what I've heard is true. Are you in here for murder?"

"Yes," the woman said, glancing in Carla's direction dismissively.

"Did you do it or were you wrongfully convicted?

"I did it."

"Do you just like killing or was there a reason that you did it?"

That's when the woman really looked at Carla, examining her. Her hazel eyes bore into Carla's like a drill bit making a hole. "I had a reason and enjoyed it only so far as knowing that he would never do to another soul what he did to me repeatedly."

"You killed your husband?" She nodded. "I'm sorry that you're here," Carla said and climbed up on her bunk.

It didn't take long for them to build a friendship. Carla didn't see Sandra as a freak of nature for killing her husband. If Carla had been courageous, she would have killed Monster.

After Carla was released, she put everything Sandra taught her to use and though they didn't write letters or communicate, Carla put money on Sandra's books every month until she passed away three months ago.

Chapter Thirty-Three

Someone knocked on the door to her office on Wednesday afternoon, just as she got off the phone. "Come in," Carla called out.

Maria entered holding a large vase of roses. "For you," she said sitting them on the desk. Carla grinned and stood, pulling out the card. "So, you've got a man, huh?"

Carla didn't answer. She read to herself what was written on the card.

~

To be with you, that's all I want.

Terry.

~

"Fine, don't share, but that smile says it all," Maria said leaving her office.

She dialed Terry's number. "I just got your flowers," she told him when he answered. "Thank you. They are lovely."

"So are you," Terry said as Carla's phone beeped.

She glanced at it and saw Pierson's number. "Hey Pierson's calling on the other line. I have to go. Have a safe flight, and I'll talk to you later."

"Bye Sweetheart."

Carla hit the second line. "Hello."

"I'm sorry. I couldn't do it. I tried, but I couldn't do it." The words rushed out if his mouth, and he continued to talk, uttering the same words repeatedly.

Carla's heart raced. "Baby, what's wrong? Tell me what's going on."

"I thought I could make things better, but I just froze."

"Pierson!" Carla shouted. "Breathe, just breathe. Where are you?"

There was a bit of heavy breathing. "I'm at the McDonald's on Lando and Park across from the Walgreens."

What the hell is he doing in that area? He should have been at school. "I'm on my way there. Do you hear me? I'll be there as fast as I can."

"Okay."

Carla ended the call, grabbed her keys and purse, rushing out of her office. "Maria. Reschedule anything on my calendar for the day," she said practically running out the building.

Why wasn't Pierson in school? What the hell could he be doing in that part of town. Nothing good could be happening there. Carla remembered those streets from back in the day. She got high and stole things in that neighborhood. He didn't belong there.

Please lord, don't let anything happen to him. Please please, don't let him be on drugs. She rushed through traffic, trying not to break too many laws. Carla called when she got close. "I'm almost there."

"I see you," he said hanging up about the same time that she spotted him. He was standing outside, dressed in dark pants and a black hoodie. She turned into the parking lot, unlocking the doors as she pulled into a parking space.

He was clearly shaken, dropping his backpack on the floor as he got in. He grabbed her, hugging her tight. Then he began to sob uncontrollably. She held on to him. "Are you okay?" He cried. "It's okay, but honey I need to know if you're hurt. Do we need to get you a doctor?" He shook his head, still sobbing. *He's not hurt, thank God.* "Did somebody do something to you?" Pierson shook his head again. "You have to tell me what happened?"

It took a few minutes for him to stop crying, but he held on to her as if she might disappear if he let her go. Carla continued to hold him, pouring her love and strength into him until he finally leaned away from her wiping his eyes. She dug around her bag and handed him a tissue. "I'm sorry," he said, wiping his face and blowing his nose.

"Sorry for what?"

"You're gonna be mad."

I'm mad right now because I don't know what's going on. "Just tell me. Did you come here for drugs?"

Pierson made a face and shook his head violently. "No. I came here to kill him, but I couldn't do it."

"WHAT?" *Calm down.* "What do you mean?"

Pierson sniffed, taking a deep breath. "I heard you tell Terry about my father. I was beneath the balcony in the garden that night. He hurt you, so I was going to get rid of him so things would be better for you, but I couldn't do it." Pierson opened his backpack and handed her a gun. "I took it from the drawer in your kitchen. I found it when I was making breakfast. I found him and followed him and when he went in the bathroom, I was gonna do it, but I froze. I went into the bathroom and just stared at him. I'm sorry."

Carla put the gun in her center console and grabbed Pierson's face with one hand, turning him to look at her. "I want you to listen to me carefully. I love you for wanting to protect me and make my life better but killing is not how you do that." Carla let his face go. "Did you consider what could have happened to you. He doesn't know who you are. He could have hurt or killed you. Your father will get what he deserves someday, but it won't be at your hands, do you understand me?" Pierson nodded. "I should have talked to you a long time ago about him, but I didn't want you to get caught up in his world. I wanted better for you." Carla hugged him again. "Did he say anything to you?"

"No."

Good, he couldn't see that you look just like him. Thank God for small miracles. "Does anyone else know about this?" She asked when she let him go.

"No."

"Good. We're not going to tell anyone about it either. This stays just our little secret, Okay?" He nodded. "I'm going to take you home now. You can tell Grandma and Grandpa that you weren't feeling well, and I came and got you from school." Carla backed the car out of the space.

"Am I ever going to meet my brother and sister?"

"I hope so, but that's a tough situation too." Carla pulled out onto the street, feeling a little more at ease. *My secrets are starting to pop right out of the closet.*

**

After dropping Pierson off, she took the gun and put it in her purse. Then she called Rooster, but he did not answer. "Rooster, this is Carla. I – need to talk to you and I'd prefer to do it in person. It has to do with one of my kids. I don't want to talk in public. If you could come by my house, I'd appreciate it. Call or text me when you can, and I'll give you the address. Thanks."

She drove home. It was late enough that there was no need for her to return to work. Just as she turned into her driveway, her phone rang. She answered it. "Hello?"

"Hey it's Rooster. I'm in Shreveport until Friday. Is everything okay? If you need me. I can come back."

Carla knew that he was at least three and a half hours away. "No. It can wait until Friday. What time do you think you can come by?"

"It may be around nine or ten at night."

"Why don't we do it Saturday."

"You sure? I can give you the number of a sponsor in Houston that you can talk to."

"It's not about drugs or me wanting to use. I just need some advice about my son." She wanted his advice because he used to be a cop before his drug addiction. She wanted him to get rid of the gun. She was sure that he would do it so that no one could get their hands on it and use it or harm someone else.

"Okay. I'll call you Saturday morning."

"Thanks Rooster."

Chapter Thirty-Four

Thursday evening after Terry spoke with his mother, he dialed Carla's number. They had shared a few texts during the day, but he noticed something was different. He hoped that the headache she told him she had earlier in the day wasn't still bothering her. "Hello," she said, sounding flat.

"Hi sweetheart. You sound tired."

"I am a little and I miss you."

"We'll I thought that we should plan a real get away. Is there anywhere that you would like to go?"

"Um – maybe Hawaii. I've never been there before."

"Hawaii it is, then. We'll figure out what will work best when I get back, but I think we should make it a week. Can you take that much time off on short notice?"

"I'm sure I can work it out." Terry heard her doorbell "Baby someone's at the door. I have to go."

"Okay. We'll talk more about this tomorrow. Sleep well."

"You too," Carla said ending the call.

**

Carla put the phone down and took the gun from her purse. She was still waiting for some sort of retaliation from Monster for kicking his ass. She looked out the window and could only see a dark colored car behind her garage. She peeked out the peephole.

Two white men stood there. Carla recognized the slightly round middle, the inexpensive, but not exactly cheap clothing and shoes. They were police. *Fuck! "Who is it?"*

"Mrs. Johnson, can you open the door? I'm Detective Cayhill with Houston P.D."

Carla quickly put the gun back in her purse and made sure it was closed before opening the door. "Can I see some I.D." The men held up their credentials for her to see. After she was sure they were the police, she said, "I go by Baxter, my maiden name, not Johnson."

"This is my partner, Detective Travis. May we come in?"

"Not until you tell me why you're here."

"It's regarding William Johnson, your husband."

"What?" She was sure that it had to do with her assaulting him, but she would play dumb as long as she could. "Has something happened to him?"

"Can we discuss it inside."

Carla didn't trust the police, but she needed to know why they had come to her. Did they know about Pierson? She stepped aside, allowing them to enter her home. Then she led them into the kitchen.

She wasn't about to entertain them in her beautiful living room.

The older, thicker man who had been talking since she opened her door, took a seat at the table. The other man stood behind his chair. "What's going on?" Carla asked taking the seat adjacent to Detective Cayhill.

"When was the last time you saw Mr. Johnson?"

"Monday. Why?"

"What time was this?"

Carla wasn't stupid. She had nothing to hide, but she didn't trust these men. "I'm not saying anything else until you tell me what the fuck this is about."

"May I use your bathroom?" The younger man asked.

"No. You may not. Don't you move from that spot." *They think I'm dumb enough to fall for that bullshit. I let him go to the bathroom and then he searches the house and "finds" something to arrest me for. I don't think so.*

Cayhill's eyes flicked to his partner for just a second. "He's missing and his mother believes that you did something to him."

Carla put her elbow on the table and massaged her forehead and temples. "You've got to be shitting me." She shook her head and then looked at the detective. "Look as much as I'd like to do something to him, I haven't. I saw him Monday because I went to his mother's house to see my daughter. We had an argument. He attacked me. There was a scuffle and then I left. I haven't seen him since."

"What was the argument about?" Cayhill asked with interest.

"He won't let me see my kids and he's pissed because I don't want to be with him."

"His mother says that you assaulted him, threatened to kill him and smashed his car."

They don't know about Pierson. That's all that matters. "He grabbed me by my hair. I kneed him between his legs, gave him an elbow to his shoulder blades and once he was on the ground, I told him that if he touched me again, I would kill him, then I kicked him in the head. I was afraid of what he might do. I backed into his car when I left."

"What did you do after that?"

"I came home, checked the damage on my car and had a drink. Look, I'm being straight up with you guys. Monster made my life a living hell for many years, but I haven't done anything to him outside of what I just told you. If he's missing, maybe you should be talking to Hammer or some of his other crew. There are plenty of people who would be happy if he went missing."

"Who is Hammer? Is Monster a street name for Will?"

"Hammer is his right-hand man, and yes Monster is his street name. His mother sent you in my direction because she hates me plain and simple."

"Where were you yesterday?"

"I went to work, and I came home."

"Can anyone verify that you were at work yesterday and here?"

It's a lie, but it's for my son. "Yes, my receptionist can verify that I was at work, but I was home alone."

Cayhill stood. "Ms. Baxter, we may have more questions for you after we verify your whereabouts. She followed them back to the door. Thank you for your time," he said as they stepped over the threshold.

Based on what they said. Will disappeared yesterday. Cayhill asked where she was yesterday afternoon and evening. She checked out the peephole, again. They were pulling away from her house. She grabbed her phone and pulled up Maria's phone number. Carla would need her to back up her story to the police that she was at work all day yesterday.

Chapter Thirty-Five

"Good morning Terry."

"Same to you Edward."

"I've got you on speaker. I'm hear with Bailey Parks, She's a family law attorney and a good friend. If there is anyone that can help your friend, she can."

"It's a pleasure to meet you Mr. Watson."

"Please call me Terry." *A few weeks ago, I wouldn't let anyone, but my family call me that. I thought I preferred Terrance. Being called Terry felt right after hearing Carla say it all the time.*

"Edward has filled me in on the details of Ms. Baxter's situation. Yes, there are several issues that we would have to address to ensure that the boy's father doesn't get custody of him."

Terry listened carefully to everything that Ms. Parks told him. Carla's situation was complex, and it would be tough, but it wasn't impossible.

"I've also spoken to a colleague about her divorce issues, and we can certainly help with that. I don't know who was handling her divorce, but a judge can enter a default judgement ending the marriage if her husband refused to sign the final documents. They should have known that and made sure that she was aware of that. We just need to speak to Ms. Baxter to get started."

"That's great. I'll talk to her about it, and we'll set up a meeting soon."

"Bye Terry."

I just hope she's okay with me sticking my nose into her personal business. He dialed her number.

It rang a few times and then went to voicemail. "Sorry I'm unavailable. Leave a message and I'll get back to you when I can."

After the tone, Terry spoke. "Sweetheart, it's me. I – want to talk to you about your situation. I may have found an attorney in Texas who can help you with your divorce and Pierson's custody issues. Call me when you can. I love you." Terry hit the end button and took a deep breath. *She may not be happy about my meddling, but she'll be happy that there is a solution.*

**

Carla's phone rang as she opened the door for Rooster. She looked at the number. *I can't talk right now, Terry. I'll have to call you back later.* She dismissed the call. "Thank you for coming."

"No problem. What's going on with your kid?"

Carla moved around him. She took the gun from her purse and handed it to him. "I need to get rid of this."

Rooster looked at her and then the gun. "What happened?"

"I'm certain that the gun has bodies on it. I took it from My ex a few weeks ago. I had it in the drawer in the kitchen. Pierson overheard me telling Terry all that I had gone through and how it has affected my relationship with my children. He found the gun when he was here and took it, planning to kill his father." She saw the look on his face. "He didn't; he said he couldn't do it. He gave it back to me, but I need it gone. How can I do that?"

"I'll take care of it," Rooster said as he removed the clip and bullets. "There's a bullet missing. Was the clip full when Pierson took it?"

"I – I don't know. Shit!"

"What?"

Carla licked her lips. The cops came by the other day and told me Millie reported Monster missing and pointed them in my direction because I threatened to kill him on Monday."

"You don't think your kid, killed him, do you?"

Carla shook her head. "No, but this is not good."

"Let me put this in my car. You call your son and ask him if he shot the gun at any time while he had it," Rooster said moving towards the door. "I'll be right back."

Carla dialed and waited. As soon as he said hello, Carla asked, "Pierson, did you shoot the gun at any time while you had it?" He paused before answering. *Fuck, shit!*

"Once, I was at the park. I shot it into the ground. That's all. I swear."

"You should have told me."

"I'm sorry."

"We'll talk about it later." Rooster came back in. "I have to go."

"Are you coming to the party."

Carla had forgotten that the party for her father was later that day. "I'll try."

"Okay, bye."

"He said he fired one shot into the ground."

"Good. Don't worry about the gun I'll get rid of it."

Before she could say thank you, her phone chimed with a text. She looked at the message. "Jesus!"

"What?" Carla handed the phone to Rooster. He read the message aloud. "Momma it's Portia, I'm using Payne's phone. Daddy's dead. Come get us. Me and Payne left the house -" Rooster didn't get to finish reading the address Portia had sent.

Carla's front door burst open, and police swarmed in with their guns drawn. "Don't move," someone said. Get your hands up."

Leave it to the police to give you contradictory orders.

Detective Cayhill and his partner strolled in as she and Rooster put their hands up. "Ms. Baxter, you're under arrest for fleeing the scene of an accident."

"What?" The world seemed to slow down and move in slow motion as she was handcuffed and read her rights. All she could think of was her children. She ignored the detective. "Go get my kids," she told Rooster.

Rooster nodded. "Don't worry. I'll get them and find a lawyer for you too." he said as they took her from the house. He put her phone in his pocket.

Chapter Thirty-Six

Terry dialed Carla's number again. It had been an hour since he left the message for her. He was checking out of the hotel and heading to the airport soon. *She could be upset with me for trying to help. That can't be it.* Carla would have told him if she was upset with him.

The phone was on its third ring when it was answered. "Hello."

Terry was taken aback by the deep male voice. "I think I may have the wrong number." *I know it's the right number. Who the hell is answering Carla's phone?*

"If you're looking for Carla, she's not available right now."

"Who are you and where is she?"

"I'm a friend and she isn't available." The line went dead.

Terry hit the send button again. "Look, I don't have time for this," the guy said when he picked up the line.

"I'm her boyfriend and I need to know where she is?"

"Boyfriend? Oh, um -Ty – T-"

"Terry," he supplied

"Sorry, she told me about you. I'm her AA sponsor, Rooster."

"Where is she?"

"Jail," Rooster said. The air left him. He listened as Rooster went on to tell him what happened. "They arrested her for fleeing the scene of an accident, but I called a friend in the department. They think she killed her husband."

"That's insane, she wouldn't kill anybody."

"I know that, but she'll take the blame for it before she'll let Pierson get in the system. They used the accident thing to get a warrant. That way they can search her house."

"What has Pierson got to do with this?"

"Long story and I don't have time to tell it. She sent me to get her other children and then I've got to find her a lawyer."

"I'll take care of the lawyer. I was on my way back to Dallas, but I'll be in Houston as soon as I can. I'll call you then." Terry hit the red button and began making calls, starting with his lawyer. He would also have to call his assistant and have her arrange a car and hotel room.

"Edward, I have a new problem. I need the best criminal attorney you can find in Houston. They're trying to pin a murder on my woman."

**

By the time they put her in a cell, Carla was beyond pissed and extremely tired. There were several other women already there. Stretched out along the hard metal benches. Some cuddled together to fight off the cold from the AC set to be as cold as the frozen tundra. Carla sat on a cement block between to younger women, thinking about everything.

She knew why they came for her on a Saturday and on a bogus charge. *Okay, not so bogus. I did ram his car and take off. They did it because they didn't have enough evidence to prove that I killed Monster. Locking me up on a Saturday slows down the process and I might not get arraigned until Monday.*

They shoved pictures of his dead body in my face, expecting some reaction. Somebody killed him and they intend to pin it on me instead of looking at anyone else. Monster had so many enemies that half of Houston could have killed him.

They mentioned DNA found near the body. Like I'm going to be scared. My DNA is already in CODIS. If they had my DNA, they would have arrested me for Murder not fleeing the scene of an accident. It's just a matter of time before I'm out of here, but I can't be too cavalier about this. They could get a conviction just on circumstantial evidence. As long as my kids are okay, I'll be fine.

She trusted Rooster to get Portia and Payne. He had her phone, so he could find her parents and take them there. Carla wasn't ready for them to know, and she didn't want them to find out like this, but the choice was no longer hers to make.

When they gave her a chance to make a call, she wanted to call Terry, but decided against it. He was on the other side of the country. By the time he got home on Monday she should have been arraigned and maybe be at home. Rooster said he would find her a lawyer and she believed him, but she did have a corporate lawyer. Livingston had handled all of her business legalities. She called him. She got his answering service, but left a detailed message about her problem.

Chapter Thirty-Seven

Thanks to the wi-fi on his plane, Terry could communicate with Edward via WhatsApp once they reached the cruising altitude. There was already a message waiting for him when he opened the app.

~

> I called a few of my buddies and Victor Cosby was only a few hours outside Houston. He's on his way into town. You'll probably get there around the same time. It was the best I can do on short notice. He'll handle everything and when you get to town you can arrange his retainer of $50,000.
>
> E.M.

~

Terry didn't care about the retainer. He wanted to get her out and figure out why the police thought she had killed Monster. He was a drug dealer and a horrible person According to Carla. Anyone could have killed him.

Being on the plane from D.C. to Houston was going to be the longest flight of his life. He'd never felt so helpless before. He should take comfort that while he was in the air, he had people on the ground doing what they could for her.

A small part of him was angry with Carla for not telling him what was happening. He sensed that something was off. She did everything but tell him about the situation. She still didn't trust him, and that hurt.

**

"Baxter," an officer called from the door as he unlocked it. Carla got up and went to the gate, facing away from it. She was placed in handcuffs. "You're lawyer's here." *Wow. That was quick.*

She was led through a series of halls until the got to a small room. She stepped inside the room, stopping to allow the officer to remove the handcuffs. She looked at the man on the other side of the table as the officer closed them in the room.

He didn't look like a typical lawyer. His suit was tailored and expensive, but the tats on the back of his hands and across his fingers gave her the feeling that he was a rough and tumble guy. He was built like a boxer. "I'm Victor Cosby. Sit down."

Carla squinted her eyes at him as she pulled out the chair across from him. "You're not from here." He had an accent.

He chuckled, "I was born here, but I grew up in London. I went to college in the states and have been here ever since."

"Rooster must have sent you. You certainly don't look like anyone my business lawyer would know. Are you one of his biker buddies?"

"Rooster? You know Rooster?"

"Yeah, didn't he hire you for me?" Carla asked confused.

"No. I got a call from Edward Mitchell, a colleague." He shook his head. "It doesn't matter. I'm here for you and that's what counts. So let me explain what's going on."

"No need. I know what they're up to. They brought me in on a bullshit warrant, hoping to find evidence to put me up on a murder charge. I figured that out when they showed me the pictures of my dead husband. I haven't said anything to them since they arrested me. I'll probably be here 'til Monday. That's fine. I just need to know where Portia and Payne are and if Rooster found them. He has my phone. I'll give you the number and you can contact him." He slid a pen and paper across the desk to her. "Do that for me and I can deal with anything that comes my way," she asked as she wrote her number down. "How much is the retainer?"

"Fifty thousand, but –"

"I can afford it. I suppose there's a contract or something for me to sign. I will not do a plea deal, don't even bring that shit to me. Not guilty is the only option, got it? Now, how much do you think the bail will be?"

"Anywhere from two hundred fifty thousand to a million for a murder charge. If this is still just a hit and run situation, the bail could be five to fifty thousand."

"Okay. I can cover the bond either way. Now let me tell you what they know." Carla ran through the details while Edward took notes.

He gave her a basic contract to sign when they were finished, stating that he represented her. "Don't worry about anything. I'll speak to Rooster and get word to you as soon as possible. I don't want to get your hopes up, but I'm trying to get you out of here tonight."

"Okay," she said, watching him put his fedora on and pick up his things. Another officer came in, handcuffed her, and took her back to her cell.

Chapter Thirty-Eight

When Terry got off the plane, he called Carla's phone. "Are you in Houston?" Rooster answered, preceding any pleasantries.

"Yes. Where am I going?" He asked as his driver took his bags and put them in the back of the car. Rooster gave him the information of where Carla was being held. Terry relayed it to the driver and got in the car. "Where are her kids and why did she send you to get them?"

Rooster explained how and why he had gone to get Portia and Payne. "They are with me now. We went back to Carla's first. They kicked the door in. I patched it so that it's secure for now, but it'll need more work, later. Portia thinks that she knows who could have killed her father. We're on our way to the police station so that she can give a statement."

"Don't let her talk to them alone. The lawyer I hired; Victor Cosby, should be there."

"I know Victor. We call him Fox. This is good. He knows what he's doing."

That makes me feel a little better. "Where is Pierson?"

"I don't know. She spoke to him before all of this happened."

"So, he doesn't know about her being arrested?"

"No."

"All things considered. I don't think he should know until later."

"I agree. He'll think it's his fault."

"We don't want that. I'll call you when I get there."

"Okay, see you soon."

Now that he was on the ground, Terry felt a bit better. Carla had an attorney, and her children were all safe. He would handle any of the financials regarding her case. He just needed to get her out of jail. Then she could tell him how all of this came to be.

When the driver stopped the car to let him out, Terry said. "I don't know how long I'll be."

"I was hired to be on call for you only," he turned handing Terry a card with his name and number. "If you want me to hang around close by, I can. Just call me when you're ready."

Terry looked at the card. "Thanks Luke." He got out of the car, walking towards the building. He dialed Carla's number.

"Hey, we're on the sixth floor. We'll be right there by the elevator when you get off."

"Okay," Terry said, going to the elevator.

The minute he stepped through the doors on the sixth floor, he knew who they were. Portia favored Carla and Payne looked a lot like Pierson. Rooster had been leaning against the wall beside where the children sat. He came towards him with his hand extended. "Terry, I'm Rooster."

"Good to meet you," Terry told him as he shook his hand. "Hi," he said to Carla's kids. "I'm Terry Watson. I'm your mother's boyfriend. I'm going to do everything I can to get her out of this mess, Okay?" Portia nodded and Payne looked at him with skepticism. "Have you talked to Cosby yet?"

"No. He'll come tell us what he knows soon."

I sure hope so. Terry didn't know what else to do. He sat down and waited. "Have you told them what you know yet?" Portia shook her head.

"I thought we should wait to talk to Fox."

"Good idea," Terry replied.

They sat there not talking, watching people come and go. They were all eager to see Carla and learn that this was a big mistake. The phone that Payne had kept ringing and he refused to answer it. At one point he handed it to Portia, "Its Gigi again. She's not going to stop calling."

"I'm turning it off. She probably has a tracker on it anyway. I'm surprised that she hasn't shown up."

Rooster moved away from the wall again, "Fox," he said grabbing the hand of a man who had just come from the elevator. "It's good to see you man"

"Same here."

"Cosby?" Terry asked standing.

Rooster introduced them. "This is Terry Watson, Carla's boyfriend, and these are two of her kids, Portia and Payne."

"Pleasure to meet you all." The men moved away from the kids and spoke softly. "Okay, I have seen Carla. She's a pistol," he said, smiling. "She wanted me to find out if you had her kids. I'll get word to her that they are here and okay. I called in a few favors and I'm on my way to have a meeting with a judge that I think is going to allow Carla to go home right away. This crap that the police are up to is ridiculous."

"I think Hammer killed my daddy," Portia said, standing up to join the men.

"Who is Hammer and why do you say that?" Cosby asked.

"Hammer was his boy. They were friends, but he and my dad have been fighting a lot, lately. Plus, the day after my daddy didn't come by, Gigi got upset about it. She called Hammer looking for him. He said that he hadn't seen daddy since Monday. That's a lie. I saw them getting in the car together. I was at the cosmetology school right across the street."

"You're sure about this?" Cosby asked.

"Yes."

"How old are you?"

"Twenty."

"Good, we don't need a parent's consent. We have to get a statement for the record before I talk to the judge. Come with me."

A sliver of hope filled Terry's heart. *Hang in there sweetheart.*

Chapter Thirty-Nine

"Baxter." Carla looked up to find an officer at the door. *What now? I hope this is about my kids being safe.* She wasn't expecting anything since she spoke with her lawyer over an hour ago. She turned to let the guard put her in handcuffs. "Turn around, you don't need them. You're out of here."

Carla closed her eyes. *Thank you, Jesus!*

She followed the officer who took her through getting her property back. Then he took her to a door and unlocked it. When it opened, she realized that she was on the main floor. "That's it?"

"Yeah. Your lawyer is waiting in the entry."

Carla wanted to smile, but a small part of her thought it might not be real. She moved slowly forward. The door closed and the lock sounded, and she realized that she was free to go. She picked up the pace until she went through the archway. She stopped and took a big breath when she saw, the people waiting for her.

Portia practically ran to her, engulfing Carla in a hug. Terry's arms followed closely behind Portia's.

Payne stood a few feet away, watching. *I can't blame him. He barely knew me when I went away.*

"Will someone tell me what the hell is going on?" Carla asked moving towards Rooster who stood with her lawyer behind Payne.

Cosby spoke first. "I went before the judge and told him about the comedy of errors that the police were using to scapegoat you into this debacle. He was not pleased. It also helped that Portia's statement gave the police a new place to look for Mr. Johnson's murderer. He dropped the hit and run charges after your daughter explained that you had been assaulted beforehand by Mr. Johnson."

"So, there are no charges against me at all."

"No. Not one."

Carla nodded her head. "Can you all give me a minute with my children?" Terry kissed her forehead and moved closer to the door with Rooster and Cosby. "Payne, I know you don't remember me. You were two years old when I went away, but I – love you and even though I wasn't front and center for your life, I've never stopped loving you. I'm – sorry about you losing your father. I know that you probably loved him. I'm glad that you came with your sister. Millie isn't going to be happy about it." She looked at them both, touching their faces. "You're old enough to decide for yourself if you want to have a relationship with me, and there is nothing your grandmother can do about it. I want to spend time with you and get better acquainted. What do you think about that?"

Portia wrapped her arm around Carla's waist smiling and nodding at her brother. "That'll be cool," Payne said.

"Great, because I have something else to tell you." Carla took a deep breath. "You have a younger brother. Pierson. He lives with my parents. He's sixteen and I'd like for you all to meet."

"Right now?" Payne asked with wide eyes.

"How about tomorrow? I want to take a bath and eat."

"Can we stay with you? I don't want to deal with Gigi," Portia said.

"Of course, you can. Is that okay with you?" She asked Payne. He nodded, smiling. "Come on. Let's get out of here. I want to wash the stench of jail off me."

She took a few minutes to thank Cosby and Rooster again for all they had done as Portia, and Payne sat in the car waiting for her and Terry. Cosby left after she thanked him. "Rooster, I can't thank you enough for looking out for me and my children. I know that by asking you to take care of that one issue, I overstepped, but I didn't know what else to do."

"It's okay. I have sons too. As a parent I know where you were coming from, and don't worry. I'm still going to handle that issue for you."

"I need to thank you for finding Cosby too. I didn't think it would be this easy to get out of this mess."

"I didn't hire Fox, Terry did. He called while I had your phone. I told him what was happening. He jumped right in and told me to take care of the kids and leave the lawyer to him."

"Then how do you two know each other?"

"He's a biker. We met through our motorcycle clubs."

"That explains the tattoos."

Rooster handed her the cell phone. "I'm going home, but you call me if you need anything." He hugged her and waved to Terry who stood beside the car a few yards away.

Chapter Forty

"Goodnight," Carla said to Portia and Payne as she closed the door to her bedroom. She turned leaning her back against the door. Tomorrow afternoon her children would meet, beginning a new chapter of their lives. One that didn't include any more secrets.

Pierson sounded excited when she called him in the car. Carla also spoke to her mother and father, but she only told them that she was sorry for missing the party, and that she would explain when she came by to give her dad his gift.

"I ran you a bath," Terry said coming out of the bathroom."

Carla smiled. "Thanks, but before we get to that," she said crossing the room. She stopped in front of him. "I want you to know how much it means to me that you came to my rescue tonight."

Terry wrapped his arms around her waist, kissing her. "I want to know why you didn't tell me what was happening," he asked when they separated.

"I told you – I – have a hard time trusting people. Plus, I had no way of knowing it would all lead where it did." She slipped out of his embrace and began removing her clothes. "I do everything I can to protect the people I love even if it means not telling them everything."

"Are you saying that you love me?"

"Duh," Carla said dropping her clothes in the hamper outside the bathroom door before going into the bathroom. She got in the tub, sighing as she sank down in the nearly scalding water." Terry came in leaning his hips against the counter, smiling broadly at her. "Why are you looking at me like that?"

"Because I never thought you would say it." He folded his arms across his chest. "I didn't think you even felt that way for me."

Carla used her hand to move the sudsy water of her still dry shoulders and neck. "Well, I do, but don't make a big deal out of it. We love each other. Let's just enjoy what we have and let the rest take care of itself, Okay."

"How do you know that I love you? I've never said it to you?"

"Yes, you have, a lot actually. You just don't know it. You talk in your sleep. Every time you cuddled with me you kissed my shoulder and said, 'I love you, sweetheart. You also said it on the message you left about finding a lawyer for my kids custody and divorce."

"No I didn't. I don't talk in my sleep."

"Yeah, you do. You've been saying it since the night that I told you everything. I didn't believe you at first, but then I realized that it had to be the truth for you to say it unconsciously without thought or reason."

"Have you changed your mind about marriage?"

"No. I love you, but I don't need a certificate or a ring to show it. I like things the way they are. Two months from now, we could be fighting more than fucking. Let's just stay in the slow lane, Okay?" *I'll have to tell Tanya that there are other things that seem to run in the Watson family. They believe in locking it down quick fast and in a hurry.*

**

While Terry counted himself as lucky in the big scheme of things, he didn't want to leave things the way they were. He wanted her to love him enough to marry him, to be a family with him and her children. *Whoa! Did I just think that? I never wanted kids before. Well, it's not like these are the pooping in their pants, crying all night kind. Her kids are pretty much adults.* He smiled. *I want to be a family man, but only if Carla and her kids are my family.*

I barely know any of them, but their mother is an extraordinary woman. I knew that the moment we met.

"Are you going to stand there grinning at me all night?"

"No. I'm going to get naked and wait for you in the bed. I want some chocolate covered cherry before I go to sleep," Terry told her, leaving the bathroom. "Hurry up, sweetheart."

**

Terry wrapped his arm around Carla, kissed her shoulder. "I love you, sweetheart, and I'm wide awake."

Carla giggled. "I love you."

"I don't like that you don't want to marry me, but I'm willing to compromise."

Carla turned to face him. "What kind of compromise are we talking about?"

"We could live together. Roman and I want to add a distribution division to the company. You could run it."

"You want me to move to Dallas and live with you, and work for your company. What about my children? We have just -"

Terry placed his finger of her lips. "I want them to come too. I would never try to come between you and them. I have a huge home and I can provide for you all. If you don't want to work with me, you can do whatever you want. I'll support you however I need to."

Carla looked at him in the darkness. "It's too fast. I need you to be patient with me. Can you do that and let me think this through?"

Terry kissed the tip of her nose. "Of course."

"Thank you."

Chapter Forty-One

When Carla woke, she was alone in the bed. She showered and dressed. It was after twelve. In a few hours she would take her children to her parent's house to introduce them. Thinking of her parents made her think of Millie.

As much as she hated that woman, she couldn't let her worry about Portia and Payne any longer. Carla left the bedroom and found Terry in the kitchen with Payne and Portia the same way she had found him with Pierson. "Please don't tell me your making pancakes that look like us."

Terry laughed, but the kids looked at her as if she were crazy. "No, I was teaching them how to make a frittata."

"Okay," she said sitting down. "You guys need to call Millie and let her know that you are okay. I don't want her reporting me as a kidnapper or something."

Payne held up his phone. "I already did. I called her last night."

"We," Portia corrected.

"What did she say?" Neither of them wanted to repeat it. They both made faces. "That good, huh?"

"I told her that you would call her later. She seemed pretty calm after I told her about Hammer and everything."

"She's okay with you being with me right now?"

"She wasn't happy, but I pointed out that we are both over 18 and she seemed to take it well."

"Okay. I'll deal with Millie later."

"Who's ready to eat?" Terry asked putting food on plates and passing them out.

**

Carla straightened her spine and blew air out of her mouth as she knocked on the screen door to her parent's house. It only took a few seconds for the door to open. Pierson opened it, grinning from ear to ear. "They're here!" he yelled over his shoulder.

"They?" Her mother yelled from the back of the house. "Go get your grandpa, he's in the shed out back, tinkering," she said coming towards them as they entered the house. "My, my you did bring some folks with you. Come on into the living room and have a seat." Everyone sat down. "Hey sugar," she said hugging Carla. The back door slammed. "Pierson, what have I told you about slamming my doors?" Shelia chastised her grandson as he came into the room.

"Sorry, grandma," Pierson said coming back into the room.

Carla was still standing when her father came into the room. "Wow, I wasn't expecting this many guests." He hugged Carla.

"Dad, this is the man I'm seeing, Terry Watson."

Terry stood to shake his hand. "Did you say Watson?"

"Yes sir," Terry answered for her as he gripped the older man's hand.

"What are the odds of that Shelia?"

Carla and Terry looked at each other and then back to her parents. She realized now that they had put two and two together. "Terry is Carl's older brother."

"Alright, I'm not crazy then," her father said smiling.

"Dad, you and mom should sit down. I have something to tell you.

"Aren't you going to introduce the rest of your people?"

"Yes. That's what I was going to do." Carla said. "These are your other grandchildren, Portia and Payne."

'Other grandchildren?" Her father asked while her mother's hands flew to cover her mouth.

Carla told them about marrying Will and that he was abusive. "That's why I asked you to take Pierson. I didn't want him raised like that. I thought I had lost Portia and Payne, but now we don't have to have secrets anymore."

Shelia cried, pulling the children to their feet, hugging, and kissing all three of her grandchildren. Then she took them to the kitchen. She insisted on feeding them.

Her father took it all in without saying much. When his wife left the room. He looked at his daughter holding Terry's hand. "Well, young man, do you plan to ask for my daughter's hand in marriage like your brother did with Eden?"

"What?" Carla asked, mouth hanging open.

"Yeah, I like Carl. He's not perfect and owns up to his mistakes and I can see that he loves my baby girl. Pretty much the same way I think you loved Carla."

"I would love to do that, but Carla and I – are taking it slow and easy," Terry said, squeezing Carla's hand.

Her father nodded. "Okay. I can respect that. Would you mind giving me a moment alone with her? If you go straight back you'll run into the kitchen."

"Not at all," Terry said, getting up.

Carla waited while her father rubbed his hands together, mulling over what he wanted to say to her. *I can't believe he still does that.*

When he was ready to speak, he looked her in the eye. "I'm glad that you seem to have found some peace, finally. You are special, always have been. 'For even the son of man did not come to be served, but to serve, and to give his life as a ransom for many,' Mark ten-forty-five. You have always been a servant, even when you strayed off the path. You paid the ransom that set those kids free." Her father got up from his chair and went to her. Taking her hands, he pulled her to her feet, wrapping his arms around her, stroking her back like he did when she was little. "I've never stopped praying for you to find peace and happiness."

Tears flowed from her eyes as Carla realized that she could now live in peace without fear of losing one thing or another. Her children accepted her. Her parent's welcomed her fully, and the man she loved, stood with her at the worst time of her life. She let all of the stress she'd been holding go.

When her father let her go, she thought she might collapse. *I had no idea how tightly I was bound by my secrets.* She breathed deep, smiling as she wiped her eyes.

"Now, tell me what it is about these Watson men that you girls find so irresistible?"

Carla giggled, "I can't speak for my sister and my cousins, but Terry reminds me of you in a way."

"I guess I better get to know him then," he said kissing her cheek and heading towards the kitchen.

She never thought about it until her father asked, but Terry had the strength her father had. He'd never given up on the possibility of being together, not even when things could have fallen spectacularly to pieces. She looked up. *It wasn't luck. It was you, God. Thank you."*

Her father stopped in the hall, turning back to her. "I expect you and my other grandbabies to be sitting with your mother and Pierson next Sunday. No more sneaking into the balcony after service starts."

Carla's mouth hung open before she snapped it shut and followed her father. *Parents don't miss anything, do they?*

Chapter Forty-Two

Terry sat in the car with Pierson, Portia, and Payne. They eagerly watched Carla and Millie talking in front of Millie's house. "How do you think it's going?" He asked them, peeking over his shoulder to see if they were as interested as he was.

"Well, they haven't started swinging on each other. That's good, right?" Pierson asked everyone.

"And Gigi's not yelling and pointing her finger at her."

"Yeah, but she just crossed her arms, like she's about to go off," Payne added.

"She's looking this way," Terry said, still glued to the women. "Your mom is waving for you to go."

Terry wasn't sure if he should get out too. They hadn't discussed it. Carla had only said she wanted to speak to Millie alone before the kids got out. It only took a minute for Millie to grab Pierson and hug him. Carla watched and glanced in Terry's direction.

Then all three children hugged Millie. Carla said something else when she let them go, and Millie nodded. *Damn it. I should have gotten out so I can hear this.*

There was another group hug. Then Carla returned to the car alone. As soon as she closed the door, Terry pounced. "What happened?"

**

"I told her that I was sorry for her loss as a mother. I then told her that we had to do better for the kids. I let her know that I wouldn't stand back and not be a part of their lives. She wanted to go off, but I explained that she had another grandchild that she might never get the chance to know unless she stopped bashing me for who she thinks I used to be." Carla backed out of the space as her children went inside with Millie. "I pointed out that Monster wasn't a saint and that she was being hypocritical. She wants to know Pierson and even though I still feel like she's the spawn of Satan, I want Pierson to have the chance to get answers to all the questions he has about his father. Even though he wanted to kill Monster a week ago, he needs information so that he can decide who he is going to be. I think he wanted to hang out with his siblings more than anything. We'll come back for them all, later."

"You trust her now?"

"Nope. I trust God." It wasn't easy leaving her children there. Whether she liked it or not, Millie was their grandmother. *Everyone deserves at least one second chance to do better.* "How long are you staying in town?"

"I don't know. I could stay a few more days if you want."

"Yes, please."

"Okay, I just need to make some calls when we get back to your place."

"I need to make a few calls too."

**

When Terry finished talking to Roman and his assistant, Carla was still on the phone. He was quiet as he came into the kitchen. "So, you're telling me that, you spoke directly to this guy?" She listened. "He said yes?" Carla listened and then did a little happy dance. "That's great news. I am ecstatic. I'll call you tomorrow and we'll get this finalized." She sat her phone on the counter and danced some more.

"Good call?" Terry asked moving into the room. She had a folder and paper spread out on the counter.

"Great call," Carla answered shimmying around him.

He looked at the papers on the counter. They all had to do with stocks. "What's all this?"

Carla stopped dancing and moved around him collecting the papers and stacking them neatly in the folder. "A brighter future."

"Are you investing in stocks? I have a great broker."

Carla held up her hand. "So do I, and he just made the deal of a lifetime."

"But it's Sunday."

"I know the market is closed, but I've been trying to acquire three shares in a particular company. Now I have an agreement that as soon as the market opens, they are mine."

"Why are these shares so important?"

"Because the give me controlling interest in the company I want."

Terry was struck dumb for a minute. "Wait, are you telling me that you are making a bid to take over a corporation?"

Carla grinned and nodded her head. "I guess I should tell you the last secret I've been keeping from you."

Terry made a face and folded his arms. "The last secret?"

"The last one."

"Okay. Tell me."

"You remember when I told you that I stole from Monster when I planned to leave him." Terry nodded. "I hid that money in the basement of my father's church. He had a storage room full of junk that he refused to get rid of. I hid the money there because no one ever went down there. I really didn't expect it to be there when I got out, but low and behold, it was. By that time, I had learned how to invest from my bunkie, which I did. I've been investing in startup companies at just the right time since I got out of prison. I'm not an employee of 3P. I own it. Portia, Payne, and Pierson -3P."

I'm blind as a bat. How did I not put that together?

"I was afraid to put my name on it because Monster would be entitled to it if he ever found out. Texas is a community property state. Even with us being separated, he could have won alimony, so I purchased it through a few shell companies the same way I've bought the stock in W.D.C.

W.D.C? It couldn't be. That wouldn't be a distribution company, Wainwright, Donaldson, and Carmichael?"

"Yup, that very one."

"I don't believe this," Terry said shaking his head, laughing hysterically.

Carla watched him as he doubled over. "What's so funny?"

Terry gathered himself and finally stopped laughing. "I told you that I got bullied in school and I've always struggled with feeling like I didn't belong or that I wasn't good enough. Malcom Wainwright, Jeremy Donaldson, and Gregory Carmichael made boarding school hell for me. They are the owners of that company. They came to me looking for help to buy the last of the shares so that they wouldn't lose the company in a takeover bid. They needed money and I said no. That's what got me and Roman thinking about adding our own distribution division. That's how I came up with what we talked about last night." Terry grabbed her kissing her. When he let her come up for air, he said, "I'm never letting you go, even if you won't marry me. You are priceless Carla Baxter and you're mine.

Kimberly Smith

Epilogue

Terry walked through the house. It was unusually quiet. For the past four months his house had been popping with activity. Carla and the three Ps had moved to Dallas when she took control of W.D.C. Distribution. He had been ecstatic when she said she would live with him.

It felt like it had taken forever for them to get to where they were. The investigation into Monster's murder took only a few weeks with the information Portia provided in her statement to the police.

Victor was the one to call and tell them about it. He called Carla while she and her children were in Dallas visiting Terry before they moved in. She put him on speaker when he said he had information about the case.

"Hold on, I want Terry to hear this for himself." She pressed a button on her phone. "Go ahead, I've put you on speaker," Carla told him.

"Hammer was the one who killed Mr. Johnson. When they picked him up, he still had the gun he used in the shooting. It took the detectives a while to get him to come clean, but when he finally told the truth he said he did it because Monster slept with his woman."

"That's a shame, all because of a woman," Carla said. "Thanks for letting us know, Victor." They were both happy to have that ordeal over with. They told the children, and everyone was happy that it was in the past.

Things continued to get better after that. Now, they were discussing merging the two companies. He didn't blame Carla for being careful to ensure that her children's futures were protected, especially when he learned that her net worth was slightly higher than his. She was better than good at business. She truly was perfect for him.

Right now, I just wish I could find them. "Hello!" He called out. "Where is everyone?" He shouted as he got to the main staircase. Then, he jogged up them. "We're going to be late."

"Carla!" Maybe she was still getting ready. Terry rushed to their bedroom. *I still can't believe that she moved in with me.* He opened the door to the bedroom. "There you are,"

Terry said walking to the balcony. It was her favorite place in the house. She was sitting on the settee; a light wind blew a strand of her hair. "What are

you doing? I can't find the children anywhere. We're going to be late to his graduation."

Carla stood up. "I told them to go early. They took the Honda." Now that they had a selection of cars to drive. She had to designate which cars they were allowed to use. She felt less stress having them taking her old car.

"Okay, are you ready to go?"

"I need to tell you something." She got up and walked over to him. "I lied to you."

"About what?"

"I lied when I said that I would never get married again." He wasn't sure he heard her correctly. *I may have just had a stroke.* His beautiful sweetheart, got down on one knee in her black Valentino pantsuit, taking his hand. *Please God, don't let me be dead or dying.*

"The friendship that we share is better than anything I could imagine or have hoped for." She paused to swallow the lump forming in her throat. "You have taught me what love really is. It's doing something as small as running a bath for me when I've had a hard day. It's the way you talk to the three Ps. It's flying my parents up here for the holidays. It's putting up with Millie when I let her come see the kids. I didn't know that being in love with someone could be so wonderful." She paused again, taking a deep breath. "You gave up on the thing you wanted most, marriage. You did that so I could feel safe and in control, but that's not fair to you." The dam broke and tears fell from her eyes. She let them fall. "I'm happy, my kids are happy. We are a family and I want to give you the only thing you've ever asked for. Terrance Bernard Watson, will you marry me?"

Carla opened the ring box in her hand, looking into his eyes. Terry pulled her too her feet wrapping her in his arms, crushing her lips with his. When he finally let her go, he answered her question. "Yes! Yes, a thousand times yes!" He wasn't aware that he was crying until Carla used her fingers to wipe his face. She took the ring from the box and slid it on his finger. He looked at it lovingly. "Do you like it?"

"I adore it." It was the most beautiful black band with black stones around it.

"I had to get something special for you. The stones are black diamonds. I didn't even know that there was such a thing. It's different and unique, just like you."

He kissed her again. "I can't believe you did this."

"We made a deal. I told you that If I changed my mind about marriage, I would propose to you. The next thing I need to do is get the tattoo on my back removed."

"I love you sweetheart."

"I know."

"You're supposed to say I love you too."

"When have I ever done what I was supposed to?"

The End of the Beginning

https://www.amazon.com/product-reviews/B09T2PFCWY

www.creativekrs.com
https://creativekrs.com/direct-discount-book-store
https://www.amazon.com/author/smithkimber

Special Announcement

Would you like to read my books for FREE before anyone else?

If you said yes click the link below to find out how you can read for free and have a chance to get great prizes for being a part of the CreativeKRS ARC Team.

www.creativekrs.com/arcteam

If you like this series and would like to read books about the Road Beasts, let me know by participating in the Survey at www.creativekrs.com at the bottom of the home page.

The first book released in this series is still up to you.
You can vote until April 30, 2022.
The first book will be released on July 1, 2022.

While you are waiting for the roar of motorcycles, keep an eye out for an update on the Watson men and the women they love.

The
Watson Weddings

Kimberly Smith

About The Author

Kimberly Smith was born in Aurora, Colorado, and raised in Dallas, Texas. Nothing about her life has ever been simple or easy. She was raised by a single parent who was visually impaired. Kimberly always had an active imagination. This creative imagination led her to a life of crime. Eventually, she was caught and served time in federal prison for a white-collar offense. During that time, she regained her love of reading and writing.

Kimberly's experiences have shaped who she is throughout her life, and she is grateful for her "federal vacation." Without it, she would not have known of her illnesses and would not be alive today. She has survived cancer. She thanks God for giving her a second chance to dig deep and understand what life is about.

Kimberly enjoys watching The Walking Dead Franchise of shows and snacking on gummy bears and flaming hot Cheeto's while letting her imagination run wild. Most of her stories have been in the interracial romance genre. With a love of unbelievable fiction, she is expanding into mysteries, science fiction, and paranormal writing.

Keep up to date on what she is working on at https://www.creativeKRS.com

Made in United States
North Haven, CT
07 April 2022

18008622R00124